1,000,000 Books

are available to read at

---

www.ForgottenBooks.com

Read online
Download PDF
Purchase in print

ISBN 978-0-243-19652-4
PIBN 10788465

This book is a reproduction of an important historical work. Forgotten Books uses
state-of-the-art technology to digitally reconstruct the work, preserving the original format
whilst repairing imperfections present in the aged copy. In rare cases, an imperfection in
the original, such as a blemish or missing page, may be replicated in our edition. We do,
however, repair the vast majority of imperfections successfully; any imperfections that
remain are intentionally left to preserve the state of such historical works.

Forgotten Books is a registered trademark of FB &c Ltd.
Copyright © 2018 FB &c Ltd.
FB &c Ltd, Dalton House, 60 Windsor Avenue, London, SW19 2RR.
Company number 08720141. Registered in England and Wales.

For support please visit www.forgottenbooks.com

1 MONTH OF
FREE
READING

at

www.ForgottenBooks.com

By purchasing this book you are eligible for one month membership to ForgottenBooks.com, giving you unlimited access to our entire collection of over 1,000,000 titles via our web site and mobile apps.

To claim your free month visit:

www.forgottenbooks.com/free788465

* Offer is valid for 45 days from date of purchase. Terms and conditions apply.

English
Français
Deutsche
Italiano
Español
Português

www.forgottenbooks.com

Mythology Photography **Fiction**
Fishing Christianity **Art** Cooking
Essays Buddhism Freemasonry
Medicine **Biology** Music **Ancient
Egypt** Evolution Carpentry Physics
Dance Geology **Mathematics** Fitness
Shakespeare **Folklore** Yoga Marketing
Confidence Immortality Biographies
Poetry **Psychology** Witchcraft
Electronics Chemistry History **Law**
Accounting **Philosophy** Anthropology
Alchemy Drama Quantum Mechanics
Atheism Sexual Health **Ancient History**
Entrepreneurship Languages Sport
Paleontology Needlework Islam
Metaphysics Investment Archaeology
Parenting Statistics Criminology
Motivational

LOLA:

A TALE OF THE ROCK.

BY

ARTHUR GRIFFITHS,

AUTHOR OF

"THE QUEEN'S SHILLING," "MEMORIALS OF MILLBANK," ETC. ETC.

IN THREE VOLUMES.

VOL. I.

LONDON:

SMITH, ELDER, & CO., 15 WATERLOO PLACE.

1876.

823
G 875l
1876
v. 1

TO

ALL OLD FRIENDS AND COMRADES

OF THE

HAPPY DAYS SPENT UPON THE ROCK

OF GIBRALTAR

I INSCRIBE THIS BOOK.

CONTENTS OF VOL. I.

LOLA:

A TALE OF THE ROCK.

———◆———

CHAPTER I.

DISEMBARKING.

IT was the fierce month of July, and the Rock of Gibraltar, crouching low, as it might be, to cool its heated flanks in the waters that lap its base, lay like a lazy lion asleep in the dog-day heat. This Rock—Tarik's Rock—it owns a dozen names. Calpe to the ancients, or right-hand pillar of Hercules; "Gib" to the subalterns and soldiers, who hate its "sentry-go;" to Jack Tar "the mighty big stone;" to the natives, "scorpions" so called, who are bred and

VOL. I. A

born upon the narrow strip of habitable land
that has gathered together at its base, it is
La Plaza—the fortress, the strongest place in
all the world. Beyond its barrier gates, the
Spaniards, its past possessors, yearning to
own it once again, christen it *El cuerpo*, "the
corpse," for there, in the paling light of evening it floats, for all the world like the body
of a dead man with head thrown back after
the last throes, with one knee bent, the other
straight out, stiff, stark, stone cold.

It knows as many moods as it has names.
The silent hills across the bay, and the sum-
mits, vermilion tinged, of the Bermeja Sierra,
have stood and watched it all these years,
and could tell endless tales of all its changing
glories. How at times it might be a huge toy,
a Noah's ark set in a sea of mother-of-pearl;
how when the east wind comes with its mists
and vapours, drawn from all the long length
of Mediterranean waters, the summit is half
extinguished by a nightcap of dark dense
cloud; how when the smoke of its hundreds
of cannon curls in fantastic wreaths around its
sides, it raises its head, thus proudly garlanded,

as might an ancient warrior upon the day of his triumph.

Now it is of metal; its hard, harsh outlines might be of bronze, or a smouldering cinder-slag half consumed in the blazing heat. The sun has worked like an opiate to lock up every eye. The semi-Spanish natives doze through their midday siesta; the dogs forget to bark; that flag, which has so often braved the battle and the breeze, droops with almost cowardly indolence against its staff; the very sentries beneath their awnings survey the piled-up shot, the heavy guns, and the pow-der-houses committed to their charge with a benevolent haziness of vision, which will degenerate ere long into an unmistakable snore, unless roused by the rounds, or the terrible town-major, for ever on the watch.

But there is one man quite wideawake. Bombardier Brigstock, as he sweeps the Straits with his glass from the upper signal-station, is very much awake. Here at this high level he catches a sniff of air from the Mediter-ranean, and his occupation is not the severest toil. His telescope is on a rest, with the

swivel well greased; his pipe is alight and
drawing well; hard by in the signal-house a
cool brew of shandy-gaff awaits his nod. He
is an important person upon the Rock. It
is he who settles the time, who Joshua-like
controls the sun, firing from his standpoint
in the clouds the signal-guns that open and
close the fortress gates. He is learned, too,
in shipping; knows every rig and build; can
swear, when miles away, to the "Mail,"
whether homeward or outward bound; can
tell at a glance the swift *faluchas* that bring
the muscatels from Malaga, from the stealthy
smuggling craft with their long sweeps and
lateen sails, and laden with mysterious cargoes
styled "sundries" in the Shipping Gazette of
the place. Ships of war, foreign or imperial,
yachts, traders, he knew them all, and for
all had the appropriate signal ready at hand.
One only he had never run up the halyards;
but this too he hoped to signal some day
before he died—"An enemy's fleet in sight."
The flags were there; would they ever be
used? Perhaps he felt that, up where he
was, upon the top of the Rock, was the safest

spot in a bombardment: he was a gunner himself, and knew that nothing short of sky-rockets could touch him.

"That's her!" he says suddenly to Bill Jakers, his assistant, who runs the bunting up, the bulgy black balls of canvas, the pendants, and fires the warning guns. "That's her!" he repeated, shutting up his telescope with a "click." "Run up a blue burgee on the lower yard. A gallus long time she's been a-doing of it. But what can you expect from a 'trooper?' Troop-ship 'Upnor Castle;' Royal Halber-diers aboard. I see them swarming about the deck like little red ants."

And now all at once the town below is startled into life. By degrees a crowd of people are on the move. First one orderly, then another; a staff officer, mounted, trots sharply out to "the South;" next come commissariat waggons drawn by mules; fatigue-parties of soldiers in white jackets; ladies, English and native, some in bonnets, some in mantillas, all with fans and sunshades; and, last of all, a motley throng of hotel-touts, Jew dealers, enterprising shopkeepers, striving to be first

in the search for the favour of these patrons
newly arrived.   Theirs is a common destina-
tion—the New Mole Gate.

While the crowd increases here, and all with
honeyed accents seek to win their way past
the officer of the guard to the Mole below,
the " Upnor Castle" glides slowly onward
to its moorings.   The sea is calm, the landscape quiet; across the bay runs a jagged
line of purple mountain-tops, distant hills, hills
nearer at hand, then gentle slopes, ending at
last in sandy flats around the white town of
Algeciras, lying quite upon the water's edge.
The surface of the water is smooth and bur-
nished, a very mirror, reflecting details the
most minute—the beacon with its egg-shaped
top at the end of the Mole; the masts of the
advancing ship, and round them a maze of
intricate entanglement of rope, cable, and
block ; the passing shadows even of the sea-
birds as they flit by in rapid flight, skimming
the surface in search of prey beneath.

On board the troop-ship there was far less
excitement than on shore.   Of the soldiers
in the forepart, some lounged lazily over the

side, staring at the big brown Rock, trying to count up the sentries whose bayonets now and again glistened in the sunlight; others gathered round Jack Hanlon, who had " put in his time" with the " Secondy Queen's" years back at Gibraltar, and had learnt then by heart where the grog-shops lay, and the price of liquor. Grog and the number of nights in bed—off guard, that is to say—are first among a soldier's thoughts on reaching a new garrison. The Halberdiers were mostly in their shirt-sleeves smoking. No orders had been given yet for disembarkation, though every one was ready. The white belts, reeking of new pipe-clay, festooned all the rigging around, bearing thick as fruit great black pouches, bright buttons, and brass-work. The squad-bags were filled, the greatcoats folded and strapped upon the packs. Five minutes after the bugle-call, every man could fall in in full war-paint, ready to march on shore.

Aft upon the poop a group of officers discussed with more animation the Rock that was to be their home for the next few years.

Among them were one or two ladies, officers'
wives; and all were listening to old Honeybun, the paymaster, who gave himself out as
an authority upon the new station.

"Mr Company Manners," they called Honeybun in the regiment, because he always minced
his words and tried to talk fine. It was odd
to hear the *h*'s go astray like unbroken colts,
in spite of his efforts to harness and drive
them in neat-turned speech. But there was
nothing beyond Honeybun when he was in
a select society that believed in him; no
accomplishment he had not mastered, no
branch of his education that had been neglected; yet he made the strangest hash of
Latin quotations, and his French was the
subalterns' joy on a dull afternoon. He
had risen really from the ranks; he could
not deny that. But great men had sometimes risen from even lower beginnings;
and Honeybun, by talking vaguely of his
birth and parentage, and of the affluence
in which he had been cradled, gave the
public to understand that he could dazzle them
not a little by drawing back the veil that hid

the mysterious past. The haziness of these distant, undefined reminiscences were, in artistic phrase, suggestive : details might be filled in according to the imaginative powers. Old Gotham, the pioneer-corporal, was Honeybun's *bête noir :* they had been drummers together, but the one had far outstripped the other, and the least fortunate detracted when he dared from his professional superior's merits, swearing, in strict privacy at the canteen, that Honeybun had learnt all he knew of manners and gentility when body-servant to Mr George Fairfax in another regiment. Nor did Honeybun deny that he had soldiered years before elsewhere than in the ranks of the Halberdiers. He was fond of talking of his old " cawr ; " using the word *corps* because "regiment" sounded to him more meagre in meaning. He was full of tales of the days when " my cawr " lay at Belgaum and Bellary and Moulmein, although, to listen to him, he might have been its colonel, instead of a simple private in its ranks.

This is how he spoke of Gibraltar.

"I mind it well—gay and glorious. Them's
the words, boys. Sherry white wine—Man-
zanilyer they calls it—in every tap, and poor
Os by the score."

"Poor Os ?" asked some one laughing.

"That's Spanish Casteylarno for cigars. For
all your learning and schooling, it seems you
can't speak every language, young squire."

"Cigars and cogniac—that's your idea of
life isn't it, Company ?"

"Beer and pipes, I should say," added
another voice.

"*You've* hardly left off milk," retorted
Honeybun in high dudgeon.

"Don't get angry, Company," said young
Wriottesley. "Tell us more of the Rock.
What else is there besides wine and tobacco ?"

"There's bull-fights, *corriders*, and fruit, and
masked balls, and red mullet, and beauties in
black silk "——

"All on the Rock ?"

"There, and somewheres else. In the
towns round — Malaga, Cadiz, Sevillyer lá
Belliya, Ronder "——

"That's short for *rendezvous*, I suppose ?"

"Most likely," replied Honeybun innocently. "It's where you go for the Fair."

"Do you walk?"

"Walk!" with the utmost contempt. "No; ride. You get on your mule, and you trot across the Sairey."

"Sahara, you mean—that's on the other side, in Africa."

"I don't mean the other side, Mr Cockey-wax. I know what I'm talking about. I said See—airey. That's Casteylarno for mountains."

"And did you often go?" asked Mrs Sproule, a fair-haired, neat-looking woman, who was leaning back in a cane-bottomed chair.

"I was always a-going. My mast"——' Honeybun checked himself suddenly.

"Your what, Mr Honeybun? Mast——?" went on Mrs Sproule quickly, with malicious interest.

But further conversation was at this moment checked by a sudden uproar at the Mole. Frantic cries of "Stop him!" "Stop him!" "Throw him overboard!" rose in many accents from many tongues, while others of those on shore pointed to a man who was climbing the side of the " Upnor Castle."

The intruder, to whom attention was thus called by others envious of his enterprise and good fortune, was nothing daunted by the shouting, and labouring upward, gained at length the deck, to find himself in the arms of the sentry at the gangway. Here he met with rather a rough reception.

" Now, Johnny, what you want ? " shouted the soldier. People of small education, speaking to a foreigner, fancy they must use a broken language or bellow; as if ignorance of tongues was to be surmounted like deafness or by baby-talk.

" What you want? No comee here—no permittee."

But the newcomer would not understand, and made as though he would push past.

" No one is allowed on board, I tell you," said the sentry waxing wroth. " You must go back where you come from. Them's my orders. Go back—else I'll make yer."

" No, Señor, no; for the love of heaven,

no," said the old man (he was quite old, and very poorly dressed), cringing low and speaking in weak, whining tones.

But he could not wheedle the stern sentinel into forgetfulness of his duty.

"I tell you you shan't come by. Go down into your boat again, will you or won't you? Must I make you? then "——

A scuffle ensued. For half a second the old man struggled helplessly in the soldier's iron grasp, and then was borne heavily to the ground.

"For shame, man! he's old enough to be your father," shouted a strong youthful voice from among the group, by this time attracted to the spot; for most of the loungers on the deck had come to the end of the poop, and were looking down upon the scene, more or less indifferent though amused. If none save chivalrous Frank Wriottesley seemed disposed to raise a protest against the soldier's conduct, it was because—trained in the strict school of military discipline—they recognised the sacred functions of a sentinel and the orders entrusted to him.

But Frank Wriottesley spoke. Nay, more; jumping hastily down the companion-ladder, he went forward to interpose personally for the protection of the old man.

"Hands off!" he said again pretty sharply to the sentry. "The man's done no harm; let him go."

"My orders was to let no person aboard unless passed by an officer, sir."

"Let him alone then. You were not ordered to assault people. I'll answer for him;" and with that Frank lifted the old gentleman to his feet, and lent him gently against the bulwarks.

"Who are you? What do you want?" asked Frank.

The other for reply began fumbling in his pockets, with such evident haste and anxiety, that it seemed doubtful whether he did not seek some hidden weapon wherewith to wreak vengeance on the outrager of his honour. But while Wriottesley was debating whether he should seize the old man's hands, they reappeared from the depths of his musty alpaca coat bearing a bundle of cards, one of which, with a lowly reverence, he presented to his preserver.

On it was printed :—

MARIANO BELLOTA,

Dealer in Moorish Curiosities, Spanish Fans and Lace,

FURNITURE FOR HIRE—BILLS CASHED,

7 CRUTCHETT'S RAMP,

GIBRALTAR.

" I'm blest if it ain't the Viscount!'" cried Honeybun.

" Yes, 'Viscount ;' I am the Viscount, Señores. The best shop in all Gibraltar. Cigars, money, what you want."

" To think of old Viscount being still to the fore!" went on Honeybun. " He was as old as the hills twenty years ago, and here he is at his trade the same as ever."

Meanwhile the Viscount went among the officers, handing them his cards and begging their patronage. This sobriquet of his he had earned ages ago, when a certain young nobleman in a marching regiment had been his own familiar friend. So he said himself, and he was never tired of quoting the Viscount; but the real story was, that in some curious bill transaction, his Lordship had been goaded into giving Bellota a sound thrashing.

"Don't go to Solomon, Señores—Solomon Corta Bolsas; he awful jew," said the old man with each card.

He had a nasty cringing manner, and would not look you in the face. His eyes were always downcast, except when now and then a rapid furtive glance upward showed that he was not unobservant of his fellow-men, especially with such as he hoped to bleed. This Solomon he mentioned was the opposition dealer—one of those on the Mole who had betrayed Bellota's insidious attack upon the ship. There was a terrible rivalry between the two, extending to the sacrifice of a half-farthing's profit by one for the mere pleasure of outwitting or underselling the other. Half a farthing—no more. There was a limit to the luxury.

"Ain't you got one of them things for me?" shouted Honeybun. "I know you of old,

Viscount. Mayhap I'll do you a good turn for old times' sake."

"You know me? Thank you, Señor; yes, you know me," went on Bellota, jumping at the fact, and trading on it at once, not because he also recognised Honeybun, but because the statement was of value as an advertisement. "You know how good I served you—chest of drawers, big bath, fans, *abanicos* from Cahdiz, Malaga figures, Moorish trays, rugs, cigars—all you got from me first rate—no?"

"You don't remember me personally, perhaps," went on Honeybun cautiously. "I was here when the Princess Charlotte's Light Infantry lay here, nigh on twenty years ago. Do you mind that there cawr?"

"*Si, si*, Señor, yes. I have the good memory. Plenty regiments come here—plenty officers. They come all to the Viscount for what they want. Thank you, Señor. *Mil gracias*."

"Lord George Honister was our colonel in those days," went on Honeybun, addressing the company generally, and in the small voice he assumed when speaking of lords and high-mightinesses. "We drove four-in-hand"—("Company" had been inside the coach with the rest of the servants)—"sometimes right up to the top of the Rock. Up there," he added, pointing to the signal-station, a straight, steep wall like the side of a house, along which nothing short of a team of monkeys, native born, could hope to travel. "Young Fairfax used to tool the drag."

This tremendous statement drew every one on to Honeybun at once. He was assailed with a dozen questions and a dozen incredulous shouts, and no one for the moment noticed the deathly pallor that had come over Bellota's face.

"Aha! yes, yes!" went on Honeybun. "It's true as gospel. But no one could have done it like George Fairfax—the wildest slip was George. You'd seldom meet such in a month of Sundays. Up to every devilment and wickedness; horse-racing, yacht-sailing, gambling, flirting—ay, and sometimes worse."

"He bad man, damned rascal, villain!" shrieked old Bellota suddenly in a crescendo note, and then finding that words failed him in English, he lapsed into his native tongue, pouring forth, with wildest gesticulation and in furious tones, a perfect torrent of abuse. Might a bad stroke of lightning cut the dog-souled, black-hearted thief in two parts. Might the torments of a certain warm place await him, and every other two-faced, double-dealing English officer. Might he and they suffer from bad fleas; might they die of the closed colic; might a withering sickness palsy all their powers—the robbers, the shameless, the indecent, the scandalous.

So much and more streamed forth with the wildest rapidity, he being of course all the while utterly and completely unintelligible to his listeners. They, surprised, began to sheer off one by one, thinking the old gentleman slightly crazed.

"You've got his shirt out somehow, Honey-bun; he'll do you a mischief. What did you say?"

"He must be mad," replied the paymaster, who did not care to be more communicative.

But he knew right well in his own heart
why Bellota loathed the sound of George
Fairfax's name ; and he was sorry that he
had re-opened the sore by this thoughtless
reference to his former master.

And now Frank Wriottesley again interposed, and taking the old man still spluttering
forth abusive words, led him to a seat. But
Bellota shook himself free, gathered up his
hat, handkerchief, and the cards which in his
fury he had scattered about the deck, and
hastily left the ship.

CHAPTER II.

DON MARIANO AT HOME.

·THE shabbily-dressed old gentleman who had left the troopship " Upnor Castle " in such a hurry, was the representative of a good Spanish family, which, at the time Gibraltar fell into the hands of the English, had been settled for years upon the Rock.

The Bellotas were not grandees of Spain, but they boasted that their blood was as blue as the best. Their possessions were not large, but they got from them enough to eat. They were well-connected too; cousins of the Guzmans of Tarifa, of the Gazules of Alcala, the Miriñaques of Casares, the Pan-y-Aguas and the Bebe-aguardientes of the Sierra. One ancestor of the house had fought with Córtes and Pizarro in the New World; another had

helped to grill the Flemings, a third had himself been grilled by the Holy Office. The
Bellotas were especially proud of a certain
Don Joaquin, whose bravery in the Moorish
wars had won for him and his heirs for ever
a good slice of Tarik's rock; unfortunately
for the Bellotas, Admiral Rooke came and
administered to the estate, and the property
passed into other hands.

At the time of the capture two courses
were open to the natives : they might remain
and swear allegiance to the newcomers, or
they might remove themselves altogether. In
their decision upon this important point the
Bellotas were divided. Several members of
the family migrated, but Don Bartolomeo, the
head of the house, refused to stir, and when,
later, he heard how the others had fared, he
thought he had chosen the wiser part. Of
those that had committed themselves to the
intricate mountain paths and weary leagues
of waste, inhospitable land, many met their
death. To a few the neighbouring towns of
Ximena, Gaucin, Medina Sidonia, and Xeres
opened their gates, but the Bellotas who left

Gibraltar were scattered to the four winds of heaven. Don Bartolomeo escaped such sufferings certainly, but other trials were in store for him. He was doomed to see the decay of his house. Too proud and too indolent to work, he and his would have died of absolute starvation, had it not been that a lump of bread or a handful of beans give food enough for a family in these southern lands. By degrees the Bellotas sank lower and lower in the social scale, and at the time of which I am now writing, Mariano Bartolomeo Bellota of Peñaflor, in whom were centred all the honours of a failing house, had long kept a huckster's shop in a narrow *cul de sac*, and was to all outward seeming as poor as a church mouse.

That which had been long his dwelling— House No. 47, District 29, as it was styled in the official records of the place — was a rattletrap, tumbledown edifice, which seemed saved from falling only because it was permitted to lean against the house at the opposite side. The two might have been

part of a card - castle, built up by childish
hands. The street itself was a long staircase—nothing more—a succession of wide
steps, none of them very steep, yet impracticable save to the sure-footed donkeys of the
water-carriers, with their burthen of kegs
borne in a pack-saddle like a cradle. At
the top of the street rose the sheer, straight
wall of the Rock, closing the view and the
ventilation. There was not much fresh air
astray in Crutchett's Ramp. The clothes'
lines with their steaming burthens hanging
in rows forbade it to circulate; yet when
a ray of sunlight glinted across the narrow
street, the place became picturesque and
pleasant for all its frowsy stuffiness. These
very curtains of clothes, staring white as
only the southern sun can bleach them, or
patched blue, red and yellow in many colours
as Joseph's coat, gave a quaint beauty. to
the scene, which was heightened by the
red-tiled, overhanging eaves, and the nondescript attire of the passers-by—women with
bright kerchiefs bound about their heads,
longshore sailors in jerseys striped blue and

white, or real Spaniards in crimson sashes, wide-brimmed velvet hats, and suits of dark claret brown.

Here in a dingy, poky little shop, not much bigger than a pill-box, Mariano Bellota had done business for years, sitting far within among his wares, like an evil-minded spider near its web, trying all he knew to entice his customers to enter his den. He sold everything—printed forms for the use of the serjeants of the garrison, salt butter and " sogers" to be eaten by the privates and their wives ; candles, pipe-clay, tobacco, pipes, cloth, oil-skin coats, knives, pig-skins, piece goods— everything was fish that came to his net. He never sent a buyer away ; if the article required was not in his shop he would not confess to it, saying always, " I have it, I have it ; *si señor, lo tengo*, I have it in my other store. I will bring it to your worship in half a moment, or to-night, or to-morrow "—— And he bought it forthwith expressly, pro- bably at half the price he charged for it, from some brother in the trade.

From the earliest period in his commercial

enterprises, want of capital had been his most grievous need. He wanted it to increase the scope of his operations, feeling that only thus could he hope to extend, adequately, his gains. He wanted capital, money that he could afford to lie out of, to be invested in a dozen different ways—in smuggling ventures to the neighbouring ports of Spain, in doing "bits of stiff," and taking up such paper as was flying about at the tail of some barrack "kite," ever on the wings of air. To have capital was, in these early days, his constant dream. For cash—doubloons, hard dollars, "*duros, pesos y fuertes*, dollars strong and heavy"—was his prayer day and night. "*Ay Dios mio !*" he would cry, "when shall I have enough to begin?" And for this he slaved, leaving no stone unturned till he pocketed the miserable balance of gain for which his soul panted, and by which he gradually became rich.

Don Mariano was indeed of the stuff of which millionaires are made. He knew better than most people the exact value of a shilling, and, for the matter of that, of a copper *ochavo*, a Spanish coin, the fraction

of a farthing; although not a lineal descen-
dant of the peculiar people, he had the
Jewish instinct, if not Jewish blood, in his
veins. The great rule with him, as with
every successful trader, was to make a margin
of profit. For this he would toil day and
night, and walk from one end of the Rock to
the other. In search of it he bought and
swopped, and sold and bought again, making
all that passed through his hands pay him
toll. And yet even when his dream was
half accomplished, to listen to him you would
think that he was still on the verge of
pauperism, that starvation still stared him
in the face. He thrust this forward always
when making a bargain : "*Soy un pobre; un
pobre y no tengo na-a*"—I am poor; a poor
miserable devil, without a rap in the world.
And when he was chaffering with any one not
of his own kidney—with the officers of the
garrison, for instance, and the English
generally—he found this mode of speech
brought him a decided advantage.

It was with these officers of the garrison
that he was always most anxious to open up

relations, there was more money to be made
out of them. He took to letting out furniture for hire, simply to get the *entrée* to the
barracks. With admission came other opportunities — profitable purchases of cast-off
uniforms, or the household effects of those
ordered suddenly away. By and by came
occasions for lending money; at first in
small sums, then more and more as he
found he had capital behind him. From
money-lending to cashing cheques and bills
upon London, was an easy transition. The
ice once broken, his transactions extended,
till by one lucky *coup* he pocketed a lot of
money. He had had the wit to ferret out
that, although young Lord P—— was living
too fast, and always in want of money, his
security was excellent. Bellota therefore
bought up all his lordship's paper, assumed
all his liabilities, and by and by got cent.
per cent. profit when everything was paid.
The Viscount in a rage had thrashed him
once; Don Mariano did not mind. Damages
to a very handsome tune were paid for the
assault, and as time rolled on, Bellota looked

back with complacency to his connection
with Lord P——. From it dated all his pros-
perity, and from that time forth the Viscount
was always in his mouth. He dazzled every
customer, every friend, and every foe, with the
title and name of his patron; till one day he
was himself christened Viscount, and the name
stuck to him for ever.

But although money now began to pour in
fast, and already in the folds of the old *faja*,
stowed away in his strong box, more than one
golden doubloon lay hid, still did Don Mariano
follow his trade—he still stuck to the shop
in Crutchett's Ramp, and made it his head-
quarters. It was here that he had laid the
foundations of his wealth, and here he preferred to remain. Though he owned other
stores, other hands in his pay did the work;
though his money was laid out in many
ventures—in an hotel at Tangier, in the
bull-ring at Algeciras, in fleets of *faluchas*
for mysterious trade with Spain—he clung
to his old habit of touting for himself, and,
above all, to the old den in which his youth
and manhood had been passed. He dined

in his shop off a slice of sausage, a bowl of
gazpacho, a salad or an orange stew, and he
slept upstairs.

Nevertheless there were passages in the
past life of this miserly, crossgrained old cur-
mudgeon, devoted only to money-making,
which in some measure compensated for his
surliness and selfish avarice. He was one of
those who had lived through the terrible
epidemic that had swept Gibraltar like a
scourge in 1828. He had escaped himself,
but with him one child only of the seven that
had called him father. First Encarnacion
went, then Rafarillo, then Pepe. Next his
wife, patient and devoted mother, died. Three
other children followed; Dolores was the last,
but fate spared her, or Mariano would hardly
have wished to survive the rest. With what
anxiety had he not watched over this last one,
dreading each moment the symptoms he knew
by this time so well: the fevered brow, the
red, bloodshot eye, and the aching back! Yes;
Dolores, mercifully, was spared, and for her
Bellota lived. For her sake he toiled from day
to day, hoping that fortune might come, only

for her. He was wrapped up in this Dolores, the sweet, motherless child, who grew up straight as a sapling, and with all the glowing beauty of her race flashing from her big, bright eyes. For her sake had he remained a widower, dreading for her a stepmother's harshness. "Happy Adam and Eve," runs the Spanish saying, "for neither knew fathers-in-law nor stepmothers." It would have been better for Dolores if she had been subjected to some other older woman's care and correction. She grew up like a wild, wayward child, never thwarted, never checked. One day, quite unexpectedly, she disappeared from her home. Mariano, like one distracted, searched high and low; but to no purpose. Dolores with her lover had flown to England.

Rage and despair filled the father's heart, and with all the warmth of his southern, passionate nature, he swore revenge—an impotent oath, for he was powerless against the man who had lured his daughter from him. And all his anger vanished when Dolores returned, pale, careworn, dying. In that cold, northern land, unlike her sunny birthplace, she had pined at once. The seeds of disease sown among English fogs, where, as the Spaniards say, the sun is seen only through a blind, grew apace, nourished and fostered by the remorse that gnawed at her heart when she thought of the house in Crutchett's Ramp and her lonely, deserted father. Yet that father welcomed her again, with a warmth of affection that no injury could efface ; caressed and petted her as of old ; spent hundreds of his beloved doubloons seeking to bring back life-blood to her faded cheek, fruitlessly. In a few months Dolores died, leaving a tiny baby, just a morsel of flesh to keep the Bellotas of the Rock from absolute extinction.

This Dolores the younger is the heroine of our story.

Having had some experience in the man-agement of girls, Don Mariano resolved to avoid, this time, the errors that had led to his daughter's death. As soon as the months of babyhood were past, the little Lola—sweet diminutive of her name—was

consigned to the care of some of his kindred
near Ximena. A cousin's wife, now a widow,
who resided with her family at the Cortijo
de Agua Dulce (Sweet-water Farm), just a
mile or two out of the town, consented to
bring up the orphan babe. Here she thrived
and grew; old Bellota wending his way upon
an old, flea-bitten, grey horse, as often as he
could tear himself from money-making, to
gladden his eyes with a sight of the child
that was fast growing to be the living like-
ness of the mother she had never known. It
is probable that her grandfather would have
left her always at Ximena, had not the
irksomeness of the journey at his advanced
age, and the loss of time it entailed, pressed
heavily upon him. By the time Lola was
old enough to be sent to school, he fetched
her back to the Rock to enter the convent
of Nuestra Señora de la Europa, where the
good sisters were to have charge of her
education and her morals till she developed
into womanhood.

A high-walled garden, not far removed
from the road leading to the south end of

the Rock, was Lola's playground and prison, when the studies she hated were at an end. But they seemed endless, these studies. She was to learn everything the good nuns could teach her, English alone excepted. Dead, deserted Dolores, had known English, imperfectly perhaps, but enough to understand the tempting, insinuating language which had lured her from her father's house. The recollection of that terrible loss was still fresh upon his mind; his heart was as sore to-day as if the blow had just been struck, even though he kept the secret to himself. He loathed the whole class of officers, *los oficiales*, to one of whom he owed his sorrows, and with them all who owned English as their native tongue. So Lola was to have no language but that substitute for the pure rolling Castilian which in Andalucia and round about passes for Spanish. But all other "extras" were included in her quarterly bills, and among them were not only music and embroidery, and the use of the fan; perhaps if her grandfather had been admitted to the private games and gossip of the convent, he might have awakened to the fact that in spite of all his anxious forethought the girl was certain to taste of the forbidden fruit of the tree of knowledge.

She and her companions led secluded lives no doubt, but the very air they breathed was impregnated with a subtle poison which they drank in eagerly, because at their age it was like nectar after dry tasks and dreary hours of confinement within the convent-walls. Foolish girls are elsewhere to be found who doat upon the military, to whom the glitter of a button and the colour of a crimson coat are irresistible attractions. For these school-girls thus immured inside a fortress-town, there was some excuse, perhaps. Soldiers and the toys of the trade surrounded the convent. A dozen times a day its walls and quiet cloisters echoed to the measured tread of troops passing to and fro; their glancing bayonets flashed reflections across the convent windows; martial music was as often in the ears of its inmates as matins or miscrere; bugles with brazen throats, or clattering drums, saluted the dawning day or setting sun : while most evenings the breeze scented with the strong perfume of the *dama de noche*, the " lady of the night," whose flowers keep their fragrance for the dark hours, brought with it also the soft strains of some regimental band performing bewitching music in the Alameda gardens below. Already each of the elder girls treasured up the recollection of some *guapo chico*, some interesting youth whom they had seen for a moment as he cantered by, bound to hunt the fox on the slopes near Magazine Hill or between the rivers, or marching down to mount guard at Ragged Staff or on the Neutral Ground. Not a few too had elder sisters versed in the gay doings at Carnival time, with many reminiscences of the masked balls at the theatre and their partners there, of the fairs at San Roque and Algeciras, their bull-fights and their splendour. Thus was Lola brought up in the very midst of the dangers from which her grandfather devoutly desired to shield her. She even learnt English, under the rose ; not much, it is true, beyond words and phrases, but enough to talk at times in a strange sort of gibberish, the only merit of which was the music of her voice when she spoke.

Old Bellota lived on in blissful ignorance. Lola did not confess to him,—she was hardly herself aware of the notions she was imbibing. She seldom saw him, moreover; only on state occasions, when she was escorted by a pair of demure sisters to pay a visit to Crutchett's Ramp. She travelled then to the foot of the staircase street in a high-wheeled, hooded calêche drawn by a sober mule, and driven by an ancient gardener perched upon one of the shafts. Little Lola was as prim and sober to look upon as Sõr Escolastica, her chaperone, or the mule which was their carriage horse. Her eyes were always down-cast, and her pretty lips drawn together as tightly and as primly as the reverend mother at the convent could desire.

To see her then, in repose, noting the mar-vellous regularity of feature, the well-chiselled nose and chin, the eyebrows arched like a well-strung bow, the tiny ears, the beautiful pose of the head and its matchless outline— this very perfectness disappointed you. It was too classical ; too severe ; too strictly beautiful ; the loveliness of a cold stone statue, as a gem of art inimitable, but in nature almost annoyingly faultless and correct.

But hers then was the beauty of the dawn before sunrise. When she raised her eyes, when those lids with their long, drooping lashes were unclosed, it was as if upon a cold, grey, morning landscape, cheerless and uninteresting, the sun had suddenly burst forth to gladden all around with its brightness. These eyes of Lola's worked like magic upon her face, rippling her lips into a smile, and waking every feature into glorious life. To look at her then, simply was a pleasure ; and if it were possible to escape the sorcery of her face and take in other details, you saw that her hair was splendid in its lustre and luxuriant richness ; that her figure, though extremely slight, was exquisitely proportioned. In stature she was above the middle height, had hands like snowflakes, and a foot noticeable even in this land of small feet, where the *piè Madrileña,* "a Madrid woman's foot," has passed already into a proverb.

Such was Lola Bellota about the time that the Halberdiers reached Gibraltar. She was now on the point of leaving the convent, her school-days ended. Girls grow fast in these latitudes, and at seventeen our heroine was quite ready to "come out," had her grandfather intended to launch her upon the giddy world of Crutchett's Ramp. Here, at least, she would have been safe from the wiles of the men who were Bellota's aversion. Few of the English officers scaled the steep steps to Don Mariano's den. Those who wanted furniture went to his other shop in Waterport Street, and in cashing bills and usury Don Mariano did not always appear —an agent in the best part of the town did all that, although Bellota looked after the business and possible defaulters with a sharpness that proved it was his own money that was at stake.

But now the time had come for him to leave Crutchett's Ramp, if not altogether, at least as a residence. This was no place for his " little pearl," as he loved to style his grandchild, to call her home. She required something more in keeping with the education she had received, and the inheritance she might expect when he was gone. But amid the conflict of many interests, Bellota hesitated long as to the choice of a new dwelling. His desire to shield his Lola from all possible harm incited him to leave the Rock altogether, and seek a home in Campomento or San Roque. But he could not give up his business and the gains it brought him. Money-making had grown to be a second nature with him, and to have retired would have been his death. As a compromise he might have lived away from Gibraltar, journeying to and fro daily; but at his time of life he could not face such constant toil.

At length, after much anxious debating, he decided to occupy a cottage of his own which lay in a sheltered nook above Rosia Bay, facing the Straits and the west wind. Making this his head-quarters, he might from it direct all his affairs; and as business would probably call him often from home, he resolved to leave little Lola in safe hands. Dueñas are an institution in Spain; she should have a dueña to watch over her, and keep her from mischief. Tia Josefa, his housekeeper, was the very person for the post. He had taken her as a servant a year or two back, because he liked the industry and perseverance with which she hawked her fish in Crutchett's Ramp. She had served him well; and now he thought he might trust her better than a stranger. Thus was the establishment at Rosia Cottage completed. The old man, the gay, light-hearted girl, fresh from school restrictions, and the sober dueña, full of the importance of her new rank, but ready, like the rest of her class, to sell herself to the highest bidder.

CHAPTER III.

SAN ROQUE FAIR.

WHEN the time came for the San Roque fair
and bull fights, Dolores begged hard to be
allowed to go ; but Don Mariano was very
doubtful about it.

Fair-time in southern Spain is like a second
carnival—even to sober-minded and sedate
Spaniards a time of licence and extravagant
enjoyment. Every town has its fair at its
regular season, from Seville, queen of Andalucia, down to Pedro Abad with its three
houses and a church. The whole population
joins in the fun such as it is ; moving
forth bodily to take up its residence on
the very spot, under the trees of the Alameda, in the principal street, or out on the
open plains beyond the city walls. Here

they spend their time from morning till night, living in temporary shanties, furnished, some of them, with taste, while others are mere shelters built of reeds and freshly-gathered boughs. They visit from one hut to another, and are visited; the old people gossip, the young flirt; there is dancing when the sun goes down, the fan-sellers light up their stalls, and from the out-skirts of the fair, where are picketted the horses and the herds for sale, comes the tinkle of bells, a mule's shrill scream, mingled with the music of a guitar or the rattle of castanets.

All this of itself, Mariano Bellota felt, would be dangerous intoxication for such an inex-perienced child as Lola. Had San Roque, however, lain in the far-off Sierra, a purely Spanish town with naught but native surround-ings, it would have mattered less. But here, close to the Rock, it was close to the fascinations he especially dreaded. San Roque would be thronged with English officers, insolent and independent as usual, ogling every pretty face, regardless of the dueña's scowl or the knife of

the jealous lover. Don Mariano was still
smarting from the scene on board the " Upnor
Castle." Honeybun had indeed re-opened an
old wound, one never properly healed, and
ready at any moment to break out and bleed
afresh. So for a long time the old. man was
very stout in his refusal.

"They are all going," said Lola, with the
persistency of her sex. "Carmen, and Encarnacion, Aurelia, Paca "——— and she ran over a
string of names, all old schoolmates and friends.

"But Carmen Garcia goes with her brother,
and Aurelia has her own mother's sister living
at San Roque, and Paca "———   .

"And have I not you to take care of me,
abuelito mio (my little grandfather) ? "

"I ? By the love of the sainted apostles!
Can I go, and neglect my affairs ? You must
be mad, child."

"You might, for me, for one day. But you
never do what I ask you," said Lola pouting,
and with tears in her eyes.

"Don't cry, child. I cannot bear you to be
sad, though the proverb says, Never believe in
a dog's lameness, nor in a woman's tears."

"*Anda!* Go to, grandfather. Let Josefa take charge of me. Is she not sufficient? Of what are you afraid? Think you I shall run away"——

Don Mariano crossed himself devoutly, and visibly shuddered.

"Do not talk like that, Lola, even in jest," he said very earnestly.

"But it was a joke, only a joke. Think you I could ever leave you, grandfather of my heart? Have you not nursed me, and kept me, and loved me ever since I was born? I cannot forget that; never while there is breath left in me."

What had dead Dolores said? Her protestations of love had been no less sincere, yet how empty had her words proved!

"My child," said Bellota sadly, "there is an old saying, that we bring up our daughters like rose-gardens grow roses and flower-pots, pinks, for some one else to gather."

"But, grandfather, am I never to leave the Rock? *Que fastidioso!* How stupid! Must I sit here all day long in the house and in the garden, but never in the street?"

"Maids and falcons should be kept out of the strong light," said the grandfather, quoting a proverb.

"Would you have me grow up like celery, always in the dark?"

"I would have you as white and pure at heart as the celery is at the roots."

"*Ay de mi!* But I weary of this life."

"You will have plenty of fun when you go to the Cortijo, to your cousins at Ximena. There will be tertulias, reunions, dancing, and who knows?—you will be choosing some handsome lover over yonder, some tall *chico* will take your fancy, and you will never more return to me."

"Señor, *matrimonio y mortaja del cielo baja.* Marriages and death-beds are settled in heaven. Besides, I want no novio, no lover, grandfather, if he is to separate me from you."

"Young girls all say that. But wait till you meet one you like—pouf—you'd forget me as fast as they fry eggs. Why try to prevent it? I might as well seek to hedge in a plain with one pair of gates."

"*Pues*, in any case there is no hurry, there are more days to come than sausages."

"Don't leave it too long, August and harvest don't come every day. In last year's nests there are no birds left. Think now, what of your cousin Lucas?"

"I hate him. He gives me *mala sombra*, he is so dark and sour; so crossgrained and obstinate. No one dare say 'This mouth is my own' when Lucas Peñaflor stands by."

"Nor yet Alejandro?"

"That mountebank! Let him keep his love for the *mozas* (girls) he meets when the column is on the line of march. As for me, I have no taste for the life of John Soldier."

"And little Miguel? will he not do either?"

"What next? a husband of gingerbread, that I might eat him at one mouthful! He is too small and insignificant."

"You are harder to please, *hija* (daughter), than Sancho Panza's doctor. Do you think the angel Gabriel will come down from heaven to court you?"

"It is a solemn matter, *abuelo*. We do not marry for one day only, but for all one's life. I want no husband yet, I seek but to go to the fair; and to that you would agree had you not a heart harder than the rocks of the stony Sierra."

"I refuse you only for your own good, Lola mia."

"*Gracias*," replied Lola, making him a low curtsey. "I am obliged to your worship."

"So formal?" Till then they had used the familiar "thee and thou," now Lola addressed her grandfather in the third person, calling him *usted*, your worship. "So formal? give me a kiss, child. I suppose you must have your way then. '*Criado de abuelo nunca bueno*,' says the proverb. Those brought up by foolish old grandfathers like me, are always spoilt."

"No, no, no!" cried Lola vehemently, "Don't say that, *abuelito* of my soul, '*Quien no sabe de abuelo no sabe de bueno*.' No one knows what kindness is unless they have had a grandfather, a dear old darling of my heart," and Lola overwhelmed him with caresses and a dozen endearing epithets.

Of the hundreds bound to the fair the

Sunday after that was none like Lola Bellota. It is the custom for Spanish ladies to attend such "functions" in fair white transparent draperies, relieved only by a brilliant spot of colour in their hair. Lola was in the fashion, all in bridal white, with a crimson blossom just below her hair, and in her hand a pretty red fan. Old age comes on so fast in this climate, that there is an especial "carpe diem" freshness about youth. Lola was like a new bud in its first blushing bloom. The glitter in her eyes might have been the drops, still undried, of the early dew. And then her tender, youthful beauty shone out all the more by contrast with her companion. Josefa, her dueña, was fat and forty, but no longer fair. Her figure, once the pride of her maiden prime, was gone; and her face, now commonplace enough, was further injured by a layer of thick white powder assumed in honour of the day—as we wear white gloves or run up a flag upon great occasions. The cosmetic hung about that unmistakable moustache as snow clings to the black branches of a tree; and now

and again a few flakes descended to soil
the glossiness of the magnificent dress of
black silk, which it was Josefa's good fortune
to wear upon this occasion.

A *calesa* had been provided by Don Mariano,
into which, with becoming pride, our couple
mounted at the garden gate of the cottage.
In this—an old-fashioned yellow machine
hung on high wheels—hardly hidden by the
over-arching hood, they travelled at a foot-
pace, an easy prey for all who chose to stare;
and as the beach was thronged with holiday
makers, bound also to San Roque, they were
not few who wished to look at Lola, and who
did so in spite of the dueña's frowns and
muttered maledictions. The good dame had
never heard of the Medusa's head; had she
known of it she might have been disposed to
exchange it for her own powdered face, just
to punish these unblushing admirers. From
the English officers who cantered by, their
white puggerees streaming to the winds, came
not only bold glances, but one or two reined
up their horses to a walk, and kissed their
hands, speaking words not altogether unintel-

ligible to Lola ; for a girl can interpret looks and compliments, even with a limited knowledge of a foreign tongue, if not by intuition. Josefa was less fortunate with those who possessed with her a common language. At the first of the many drinking booths just where the sands join the dilapidated high road, came a torrent of chaff, as the driver of the *calesa* halted for his first whet of aguardiente.

" Are you twin sisters, gossip ? " cried one; " a pretty pair. Like as two cherries on one stalk."

" Say rather like the ripe cherry and the withered branch."

" A tin sword and a gold scabbard."

" Never trust a shoeless vagrant, nor a taciturn man, nor a woman with a beard," said another, quoting a proverb, and referring to Doña Josefa's whiskers.

" *Hijos!* " cried Josefa, exasperated, " you are as sharp as bolsters. It comes to the greyhound by inheritance to have a long tail, and to you evil-mouthed have come the hairy tongues of your base-bred mothers. As is the bell so is the clapper."

"Take care how you play with a jackass ; he may hit you in the eye with his tail."

"Grandmother, do you want a *novio ?*"

"Not one that is as ugly as hunger."

"The ugliest *olla* (soup saucepan) finds a lid to suit it."

"*Calla*. Shut up ! Nowadays the chickens crow louder than the cocks. You are wearisome as frogs, and as bumptious as artichokes. *Anda*, drunkard," she went on to the *calesero*, "forward, or here we shall find our graves."

And with that the trio proceeded. But Doña Josefa's temper was somewhat ruffled, even till they reached the last steep hill that leads up to the town.

They alighted upon the outskirts of the Alameda, where the Fair was held, which, like a wide avenue, stretches from the town itself to the bull-ring and the barracks. At one end the now busy street, whereof the grass, the growth of eleven indolent months, is fast being choked and stamped out by hundreds of bustling feet ; at the other the purple hills of Los Barrios and the Carnicero Sierra.

On either side sloped fertile uplands; dotted
with olive grove and vineyard, one way to
the Giant Rock and the shore of the Gibraltar Bay, in the other to the wide-stretch-
ing cork wood of Almoraima to Castellar,
and the blue mountains round and beyond
Ronda. Bright colours in the landscape; the
sky like lapis-lazuli; the fields of green and
gold; bright colour also and vivid contrast
among the crowds that thronged the fair. A
glut of yellow kerchiefs, crimson waistcloths,
and linen, white and glittering as snow in
the fierce bright light. Rich colour and
showy contrast everywhere—heightened by
the picturesqueness that still clings to all
in Andalucia; to be seen in the gay trap-
pings of mule and horse, in the fluttering
pennons of the lancers of Santiago, posted
to keep order near the ring, in the huge
jars of the brown-skinned water-carriers, in
the tangled rags of the beggars, halt, or
maimed, or elephantiasis-afflicted, riding their
own horses, or crawling along the earth upon
all fours. Here and there in stormy discussion a couple of dealers bargained for cattle,

corn or calico, talking with rapid utterance,
gesticulating wildly, and perchance waxing
so wroth that by and by the knife alone
will settle the dispute.   In the central street,
at the best booths, were sold fans and
brass work, tall oil lamps of classical shape,
mighty basins bigger than Mambrino's helmet,
toys, gloves, silver work from Cordova, and
Albacete knives, long murderous weapons,
with blades keen-edged as razors, bearing
appropriate mottoes : " I am my owner's
champion," " Do not draw me without reason,
nor without honour put me back in my
sheath," and so forth.   Here, too, were the
drinking shops for the sale of *vino y licores*
—wine and liquor—for those who needed
them, Manzanilla of San Lucar de Barrameda,
aguardiente, British beer, *orchata*, a hot syrup.

In the place of honour, the young men's
club of San Roque, the "*circulo artistico re-
creativo*" as they called it, had built a grand
shed of rough outlines filled up with green
boughs and stalks of maize, hung within with
bright chintz, and owning a boarded floor.
Round about this bower were clustered the

pollos, the chickens, the fast young men of the place and their blue-blooded friends.

As the time for the bull-fights approached, the crowds upon the Alameda visibly thinned. Already the hoarse uproar that comes from the impatient audience was heard plainly in the distant ring. The general public had long since taken their seats, fighting for places near the *Barandilla*, on the lowest tier, that is to say, whence they might hang over and in security insult the savage beast when driven in near the boards. To them followed now the upper classes who could afford to pay for reserved seats in the *sombra* or shade; the ladies smartly dressed like our Lola, the visitors from the Rock, the Governor-General of Algeciras, or "the Camp of Gibraltar, that fortress," so runs his warrant, "being temporarily in the hands of the English."

Tia Josefa began to be impatient to be off too. She was *aficionada*, devoted to the sport, and a bull-fight was not to be seen every day.

"*Vamos*," she cried. "*Vamos*, Lola of my heart. We shall be late, and miss the *entrada* (entrance of the bullfighters to the ring)."

"It is so fresh out here, Josefa, I think I had rather stay away altogether. I know I shall not care for the function. No, I shall hate it. It is cruel, and cruelty hurts and displeases me. Do not let us go."

"Not go! *Santisissima Virgen!* Not go! and for what did we come all this distance in a *calesa?* A journey like that to the *infierno,* to the lower regions, from which the good saints preserve me ?"

"We came to see the *jaleo;* the excitement; the crowd of people at the Fair."

"*Ea!*" replied Josefa scornfully. "Throw that bone to another dog. Tell that to my grandmother the one-eyed. We came to see the bulls, los Toros, the bulls, the bulls."

"Then go you, and leave me here."

This was, of course, a perfectly impracticable suggestion. Josefa had positive orders never to let Lola out of her sight.

The girl left to herself might get into mischief—children always got into mischief— and Don Mariano would be sure to hear of it. If Josefa was to see the bull-fight at all, it must be in company with Lola.

"How can you say a bull-fight displeases you, you who have never seen one?"

"Paca at the convent told me. She has seen plenty. They kill the horses, and there is blood all about, and danger. I am afraid."

"You to talk like that! a Bellota of the best and bluest blood to talk of being afraid! What would the *amo* Don Mariano say?"

"He would not mind."

"But Paca and Encarnacion? a pretty joke for them when they hear you came to the gates of the ring, but did not dare to enter." •

Perhaps the fear of ridicule among her most intimate associates was the strongest argument on the dueña's side. But just then an unexpected reinforcement came to Josefa's aid.

Two small girls decked out like bridesmaids passed at the moment, and seeing Lola, rushed up to her with shrieks of delight.

"Lolita! *queridita!*" a dozen pet diminutives in high notes, which soon brought the rest of the party to Lola's side.

It was the family of cousins from Ximena, who had come to San Roque for the Fair. Mother and daughter, one son, Miguel, and the two children of a friend and connection in their native town.

They all kissed Lola first on one cheek then on the other with much effusion, and made one or two complimentary remarks on her appearance, when Ramona the eldest daughter, a bold-eyed, brown-cheeked *moza* (girl), broke in with—

"*Ea! corre priesa.* Make haste, time presses. We shall lose the *entrada.*"

"This gentle lambkin does not wish to go," Josefa said, seeking support which she immediately obtained.

"Not go! *Tonteria*, foolishness!" cried Ramona.

"And why not?" asked Doña Teresa, a thin, shrewish woman, with a wiry voice and a great sense of her own importance.

"They will, I fear, disgust me."

"You have no spirit, child. This sport is fit for kings. I have heard my uncle say— my uncle who was substitute administrator of kitchen-garden refuse at the Court of Aranjuez—that he has seen the king, Don Fernando, and his Queen (may God have them in His holy keeping), at many functions. It was sport for them : shall we then make a nose at it ?"

"It is a good old sport," cried Ramona enthusiastically. "As old as the itch or the way to walk."

"You will not fear, my cousin, when I am by your side," cried the valiant Miguel— a youth some five feet high, whose attenuated legs looked as if they had been shrunk at one and the same time with the tight trousers that adorned them.

"When the bull is dead you can pull his tail," said Ramona, contemptuously. "Who taught you to *torear?*" (fight the bull.)

"I am small, but I have a stout heart, and fists and muscles ! "

"*Calla !*" exclaimed the mother. "Silence! You are like chattering magpies. Come, Lola, it is time to enter."

And in this peremptory fashion Doña Teresa ended the discussion and our heroine's scruples.

Lola when she got inside was not sorry that she had come. All her terrors, in truth,

vanished in the first sensations of surprise and
delight. The sight appealed vividly to her
senses, and made all her pulses throb sharp
and fast: for as yet the coming ghastly drama
was not begun, the curtain still was down, and
the audience itself was the only spectacle;
the wild and picturesque audience beating
time to the quaint music of the military band.
Over in the "sol," where the sun struck full
upon the crowd, was a densely-packed, gay-
coloured, palpitating mass of humanity; tier
above tier of spectators, eager and agitated,
drumming their feet against the stone steps,
chanting a long, monotonous song like a hoarse
chorus to the overture. Great fans of paper,
red and yellow, were in incessant use, repeating
the movement and the colour of the flags that
waved on the topmost walls of the ring,
against the azure sky. Hundreds of British
soldiers in scarlet were dotted through the
throng, their gaudy coats seeming for the first
time neither garish nor out of place amid so
much that was bright and vivid.

Here and there a couple (*una pareja*) of the
civil guard, the gendarmes of Spain, hovered

ready to interfere in case of a row; backed up by the bayonets of companies of infantry, stationed at commanding points among the throng, and with loaded muskets, in case some small disturbance should all at once expand into a revolution. But the people were mad with excitement, not political : they roared and shouted as do the gods at Astley's or the Surrey, only pausing now and again when the plaintive airs of the Malagueña, touched their susceptible hearts, after which they roared louder than ever. The work was hoarse, and drink-encouraging : so that through all the din the cry of the water-sellers never faltered, and the demand and sale for "agua" was never-ceasing. In the universal thirst it was as well perhaps that no stronger beverage was on tap.

The Peñaflors with Lola and her dueña soon shook themselves into their seats—not in the sol already crowded to excess, where Lucas, the eldest brother, himself an amateur bull-fighter, was stationed with his more intimate friends—but in the more aristocratic "sombra," or shade, by this time sheltered from the rays of the declining sun. Josefa

fortified herself with a pocketful of ground
nuts (*avellanas,*) took three tumblers of water
running, and was quite ready for anything.
The others found friends near with whom to
gossip, and Lola listened eagerly to their talk,
which was mostly of the coming function.
Would it be good ?—Without doubt.   The bulls
were from the herds of the widow Varela,
the best brand in Spain.   Who was to kill ?
Tato, Lagartijo, Dominguez, Gordito, who ?
—Lagartijo, of course, the little lizard, the
most rising " sword," *espada,* in the land.
Tato was no good now, since his hurt at
Villa Martin ; Dominguez was one-eyed, and
Gordito was growing fat and had lost his
figure.   Ramona said she loved Lagartijo ;
it was a sight to cure the pains, to see him
jump through the bull's horns, to do the
suerte a la Veronica, the *Volapie,* or receive
the charge as a banderillero, but seated in a
chair.

Then in the midst of it all, the trumpets
sounded a flourish, the alcalde took his seat,
and the bull-fighters entered in procession
through doors opened wide, like the full

strength of a circus company parade themselves before the fun begins.

Lagartijo has made his bow, has thrown
his gorgeous cloak to an eager vassal in the
lowest tier of seats; the others have followed
suit, and now take post and wait. The
picadors prick their sorry nags tottering
beneath the loads they carry, and snuffing
death already in the air, close alongside the
barrier; put lance in rest, and wait. The
audience expectant, with nerves tense-strung,
grow hushed and dumb. They also wait.   •

This is the supreme moment. In another
second the bull, who is raging and fuming in
his den below the alcalde's seat, will be let
loose and then——

Why does Tia Josefa scream slightly, and
put her hand over her heart? Down in the
ring below, close under where they sit, a *picador*,
padded and grotesque, in chignon and broad-
brimmed hat, awaits like his fellows the second
flourish of the trumpets and the bull's first
charge.

She recognises him.

"*Jesus!* it is my son!" she cries, waving

her fan at him.   "It is Pepe—Pepe, son of my
soul. *Hijo de mis entrañas.*   My boy, my
beloved boy ! Precious infant of my soul, hast
thou returned ? "

"Your son?" asked Lola, "I never knew you
had one."

"Yes; this one only.   Pepe—Pepe Picarillo
the neighbours called him, he was so wild.
Pepe, my monkey boy, who left me years ago,
and was decoyed from home."

She did not at the moment explain that
Pepe had run away.   She had perhaps forgotten how she had annexed his earnings,
the copper *ochavos* and *cuartos* which he
had gained gallantly at the whip's point
from the English officers galloping upon the
beach.

" And now he is a *picador ?* "

" As you see.   I did not know he was alive.
But he was fond of horses always; and now,
ay ! " cried the mother, realising for the first
time in all its acuteness a thrill of anxiety at
the danger he—as a bull-fighter—was about to
run.   " May the Blessed Virgin have him in her
keeping this day !   May the bulls be mild!"

"Mild bulls!" cried an old woman close by, "and give us no sport?" The terrible danger to Pepe was as nothing to the success of the performance. "*Ea*, I pray God they may be fiercer than wintry winds, active as a torrent after rain, strong as the summer sun at noon."

Then the first bull rushed in, and settled the question in person.

A handsome, brindled beast, with a splendid head, grand horns, stout and sharp, and not too wide apart; all strength and power about the neck and shoulders, in the hind-quarters lithe and active as a cat.

For a short second he pauses, the scene is new to him—as it was to Lola. The glare is nearly blinding after the darkness of his den; and he is dazed, astonished by the shouts of the audience. But this irresolution is short-lived: the hated colours flaunting before his eyes, the maddening cries of the spectators wake up to full intensity his fierce desire for revenge upon his enemy— man.

He charges; quick and sharp as a pistol-

shot. The *picador* who is nearest rolls over;
man and horse, the latter killed, stone dead
with a horn-thrust in the chest. Number
Two meets the same fate from these cruel
horns; Number Three also; the fourth *picador* turns tail, his horse utterly unmanageable.
To him the bull gives chase; overtakes him,
lifts both rider and horse bodily upon his
horns, throws them to one side and passes
on. The man is underneath, shaken but still
safe; the horse writhes in agony, ripped up, entangled in his own entrails, reeking in his own
gore. Number Five is caught by the barrier,
pinned there, held there, the rider falls over
at length among the audience unhurt, but the
horse—the patient, helpless horse !—has his
back broken, and he falls, as soon as the
bull has done with him, a corpse like the
rest.

Nothing can resist such a terrible fury as
this. The bull is master of the position, and
as he pauses to take breath, he might look
around like Alexander panting for new con-
quests. The ring is strewn with horses dead
and dying. Not one *picador* is left; all are

dismounted, one or two lie like logs upon the ground under a heap of bones and broken saddlery; another is being helped, limping, by the terrified assistants, out of the arena; the *chulos*, who on foot should play the bull with their cloaks, are cowed, and shrink towards the shelter of the barriers; Lagartijo the chief *espada*, and captain of the troupe, is alone undaunted, standing in mock bravado with folded arms in the centre of the ring; but what can one man do?

And now the audience which has hung, these minutes past, breathless on every move, grows mad with enthusiasm. Almost to a man, they rise to their feet and rend the air with fiendish cries:

"More horses! more horses! Fresh *pica-dors*, away with the cloak! Bravo, Toro! Bravo, bull! bravo, bravo!"

They have tasted blood, these grave, self-contained, but cruel-hearted Southerns, and nothing less can cloy their appetite now.

But where is Pepe Picarillo the while?

CHAPTER IV.

WHAT CAME OF THE FAIR.

TIA JOSEFA, who had been so keen about coming
to the bull-fight, was finding it even more exciting than she expected. The thrilling danger of
her son lent a new sensation to the scene.
For Pepe Picarillo had been one of the first
to fall in the late encounter, though with the
true instinct of self-preservation, he had man-
aged to keep his horse between himself and
danger. But when lifted to his feet he was
still far from safe, and this was only the first
act of the play. So Josefa was continually on
thorns, crying aloud on the saints, patron and
others, promising prodigally, a mass to be sung
at the shrine of St Josephine, seven *rezadas*
at that of St Christopher, and to all candles,
which would probably be provided from the
store-closets of Don Mariano at Rosia.

We have paused thus for a moment to see how Picador Pepe had fared, but there had been no pause in the performance. Fresh horses had been dragged in, much against their will, to be mounted also and spurred to death, till the brindled bull had sent in all, some ten or a dozen, to their long account. But with the glut of his passion had come some diminution of his strength. Weakened now and jaded, the *chulos* engage him with darts barbed but disguised in fringes of coloured paper. These are plunged in pairs, one on each shoulder, goading him further to madness as the sticks, rattling together and clotted with gore, hang like a bleeding necklace around his throat.

And now at last the trumpets sound and summon Lagartijo to go forth to kill.

Taking the usual bumptious oath to slay the bull, or never himself leave the ring alive, he swings round on one foot, throws his black, furry hat far from him, and goes alone to the encounter.

Man against bull. Courage and skill against brute force. Which shall prevail?

However cruel and degrading may be

called the national sport of Spain, there is
no doubt that the last or crowning act in
the drama does something to redeem its
character. It is a fine sight to see the
matador (in Spain better known as the
espada, or " sword ") stand forth alone and
single-handed to do his work. He has
special training, of course; without it, his act
would be simply suicidal. It is indispensable too that he should know his bull by
heart, and this lesson he has conned from
the first onslaught, noting every mood, and
turning over in his own mind the various
styles of play he will be called upon to
employ. But no training suffices to supply
the needful nerve. Years of practice are
not enough to keep his head cool and his
pulse quiet. He carries his life upon the
quickness of his steady eye, the sureness
of his foot, the ready strength of wrist
and arm ; but he must possess also a stout
heart.

To Lagartijo, with his intrepid coolness and
the easy grace with which he performed his
part, the task before seemed the merest child's

play. Right, left; left, right; he waves his short flag to and fro, and waits with sword half concealed the chance that is sure to come ere long. All at once he delivers his thrust, a thrust sent with lightning speed in and over the horns, a thrust so long and true that the sword-blade is buried to the hilt, the bull totters, looks slowly round with fast glazing eyes, quivers in all his limbs, and falls suddenly, dead—*Procumbit humi bos.*

Once more wild cries re-echo from every corner of the amphitheatre; hats are thrown wildly down into the ring; cigars, also, by dozens; one of a group of English officers near Lola, catching at the enthusiasm and spirit of his surroundings, takes out his sleeve-links and throws them down to Lagartijo. "*Qué se lo dé! Qué se lo dé!*" (Let it be given to him) resounds from every corner, and because the alcalde hesitates to give the bull to its killer, the whole audience of the *sol* rises to its feet, and shouts in chorus, waving their hands in unison, "*Qué se lo dé!*" till Lagartijo is seen to cut off the right ear of the slain beast, in proof of ownership, and throw it up to the officer who gave him the sleeve-links.

And now for a moment Josefa breathes freely. Teams of mules, with bells and coloured banners, gallop in to carry off the dead ; the attendants strew sand upon the ground, or dry up with earth the sloppy puddles of blood and gore ; and the spectators refresh themselves with nuts, fresh water, and gossip.

With the new bull the sport was much the same as the first, the same excitement, the same hairbreadth escapes. Josefa's heart was often in her mouth, and Lola was fast growing sick of the unvarying brutality of the scene. Not so her cousins. Miguel was loud in explanation of all details, and drew many comparisons between this and other fights.

Then came the third bull : a reddish chestnut beast, of powerful frame, but seemingly of sluggish temper. He was of the class called *parados* (halters), which are often the more dangerous because they hang back and will not charge.

The spectators at first waited patiently enough while the *chulos* strove to rouse the bull, and the *picadors* made the usual gestures of defiance, waving their lances and mocking him in derision. But still he hung back, pawing the ground, a sure sign of cowardice; and patience was at length exhausted. *Fuego!* (fire) was loudly demanded on all sides; darts with percussion crackers to explode and singe his flesh. *Fuego! Fuego!* was the cry, coupled with abuse of the *picadors*, loud and unmeasured.

"Go up to him, you cur!" cried one to Pepe.

"Go to your mother, she wants you!" cried another. Poor Josefa!

Now it is by no means imperative upon the *picadors* to go out into the centre of the ring, and challenge the bull to charge. Nor can the alcalde, who has otherwise full power to punish them by imprisonment for infraction of the rules, insist upon it. Yet the people, wrong-headed, like every crowd, called upon the chief magistrate loudly to exercise his authority, backing up their demands where it was possible, by leaning over the barrier, and belabouring the hind-quarters of the horses nearest to them. That which Pepe bestrode was a well-shaped bay, once, perchance, an officer's charger in the neighbouring garrison, a " maiden " winner, or foremost for seasons with the Calpe hounds, now, a mere bag of bones, with knees faltering and every muscle on the quiver—yet, from the repeated blows, something of his old spirit awoke, and, after a few vain kicks at the boards behind, he rushed forward—a short, halting, feeble gallop—right into the bull's teeth.

In *tauromaquia* it is an axiom that the man should never take the initiative. He who does so throws away a chance, and gives it to the bull. Pepe tried with all his might to halt his horse, but in the effort his bridle broke, and he was carried helplessly, willy-nilly, to destruction.

The bull, as if he knew his advantage, received the horse at horn point, prodded him twice, right and left, then lifted both horse and man from the ground.

Pepe lost his balance, and fell over right upon the horns.

A nice lump of excitement this for such a bloodthirsty crowd! What matter that Josefa's shrieks at her son's peril were loud and piercing? They were set down as extravagant delight at the splendid sport. What if Lola turned pale and fell back in a dead faint? Women get well soon enough of fainting-fits; here was a man about to be gored to death under their very eyes and for their amusement.

For some twenty seconds Pepe hung thus, half-way between life and death. Entangled between the horns, his body lying along the bull's back, he was from the first quite beyond help. And a sudden paralysis seemed to have seized all those who should have swooped down to his assistance; each instant Pepe's danger increased, each instant the bull grew more and more frantic in his efforts to shake himself free. At last, with one terrible plunge he threw Pepe to the ground; struck his horns at once into the quivering body of his prostrate foe, lifted

him on high, and then—tossed him half-a-
dozen yards away, to fall a mere lump of
clothes, collapsed, apparently dead.

And now a sudden awe fell upon the
whole assemblage. Here in truth was a man
of like passions and feelings as themselves
"butchered to make a Roman holiday."
There was a momentary revulsion of feeling.
Que lastima ! (How sad !) was on every lip,
as the attendants bore the lifeless body
away. Two words of pity; no more. Is
not the bull still there, in the arena, charging
like a fiend ? Call the priest for Pepe; let
the holy oil be administered if it be not
already too late, but bring also more
picadors. There must be accidents. It is all
in the day's work. And there are still
four bulls to be killed.

Naturally enough there was no little confusion in the neighbourhood of Josefa and
Lola. A girl fainting, and a dueña in
hysterics, were sufficient to destroy Ramona's
enjoyment, and put her mother Doña Teresa
in a fever of fussiness. Nor were those
seated around of much assistance. The

women became talkative, chattering fast and offering all manner of impracticable sugges- tions, and the men growled "*caramba*," or worse, because the disturbance was spoiling all their fun. The obvious thing to do was to carry Lola out. But Miguel, the only male of their party, being on a small scale, and not even strong for his size, was manifestly quite unfit for the job, though he might have been willing enough to try; and Lucas, the other brother, was at the far end of the ring, in utter ignorance of what had occurred.

Help came whence it was least expected. Frank Wriottesley, the hero of the sleeve- links, the protector of old Bellota some weeks before, had been watching the whole affair from his seat on the tier just above. Early in the day Lola had caught his eye, and he had found himself again and again returning to gaze upon her perfect face. When she fainted he had jumped from his seat and made towards her. At first the crowd kept him back, but by dint of persistent elbowing he reached her at

length ; and then saying no more than " Allow
me "——he coolly lifted Lola in his arms
and strode towards the doorway.

This forcible abduction was not taken in
the best part by Doña Teresa, though it
clearly solved a difficulty for her ; and she
followed Frank out, muttering as soon as
she got breath, strong expressions as to the
abrupt ways of the English, and their want
of formality. To call him very formal, *very
formal*, is the highest compliment you can
pay a Spaniard.

Once beyond the ring and the crowd
Doña. Teresa reasserted her authority. Ramona and she placed themselves on each
side of the inanimate girl, as she lay upon
the grass, and made signs to Frank that he
was no longer required. So our hero returned to the ring.

Pepe too had been carried out, but on the
opposite side—that nearest the fields, where
the dead horses were being skinned under
the eyes of observant vultures. Here, upon
the burnt-up, blood-bedabbled grass, he was
brought and laid out, and thither his mother

made her way when the first paroxysm of
grief was abated. Now she knelt at his head
gazing with fierce agony into his lack-lustre
eye, and calling upon him, the dear son of her
soul, the sole offspring of her maiden prime, to
look up and speak to her. Inside where the
fight was still in progress, the people roared
and shouted as before, and at each fresh outburst Josefa shuddered with pain and horror.
There is no one to pity her; the sky above
is hard and brazen, and the birds of prey
openly mock at her with hungry, bloodshot
eyes and flapping wings. Only the horse-
skinners, busy at their loathsome task, spare
her a word of compassion. But then the
padre cura, come to administer the last rites
of the Church, touches her gently on the
shoulder, and bids her be of good cheer.
With him is the doctor from the hospital,
who bends over Pepe examining his hurts;
and Josefa rouses herself to hear the worst.
But he is of opinion that none of the wounds
are mortal; and what are a broken rib or
two, and a leg contused, to one who follows
the *picador's* trade? While there is life there

is hope.' By and by Pepe is removed to the hospital in the town.

And now Josefa found herself in a terrible dilemma. Don Mariano had given positive instructions that she and Lola were to leave San Roque not later than seven that night; but how was she to go and leave Pepe perhaps to die alone? She was divided between her duty to her master and her newly-awakened affection for her son. If she returned to Gibraltar forthwith, she might never see that son again alive. In the end, after the manner of womankind, she allowed her feelings to gain the day.

Lola had been consulted, and had readily agreed. She had recovered almost immediately from her fainting fit, but was by no means disposed to face the homeward journey that same evening. Moreover, she had been invited with Miguel and Ramona to the ball at the Casino—the first affair of the kind at which she had ever assisted, and which she hoped to enjoy more than the horrible bull-fight.

It was, however, considered prudent to

send word to Don Mariano. He was likely otherwise, as Josefa expressed it, " to put himself into an eleven-guarded shirt," in other words, to become seriously enraged. A friend, therefore, was hunted up, from among the many bound for Gibraltar that evening, who was commissioned, with many entreaties, to go to Rosia and explain that Lola had met her cousins from Ximena, and had stayed the night at their request at San Roque. Josefa purposely omitted all mention of her son's accident, because she felt it might awaken Don Mariano's suspicions as to the real reason for the postponement of their return to the Rock. These matters arranged, Josefa repaired again to the hospital, to spend the night by the bedside of her son.

It happened by chance that Frank Wriot-tesley of the Halberdiers, who, as we have seen, rendered such important service, re-mained also that night at San Roque. He had missed his companions, and after dining alone at M'Crae's hotel, found himself on the Alameda after dusk, in the midst of the Fair.

It was not bad fun, he thought. There

were all sorts of games afoot. Roulette tables in plenty, at which hardened sinners gambled away the copper *ochavos* and *cuartos* (half-farthings and farthings) ; the drinking booths were full, and more than one group stood round the blaze of an *alfresco* fire, in the light of which couples danced the *olé* or *habanera*, the *caña*, *fandango*, or *bolero ;* while the lookers-on clapped their hands and sang in chorus. But this, the national method, was not sufficiently fashionable for the young bloods of San Roque, who had erected the leafy bower, already described, for the express purpose of giving a ball of the most ambitious character. This was now in progress, with chaperones, a band (of two) ladies in white dresses, young *beaux* all in due form. And here Lola, now quite well, and as merry as a sportive lambkin newly introduced to spring turf and the innocent use of its legs, danced with her cousin Miguel, listening with good humour to his extravagant compliments.

"Was your father a confectioner ? " he asks.

"My father? How should I know? Why?"

"Your lips are like sugar-plums—like scarlet candied drops."

"*Ea*—but they are not for you to taste, Miguelito."

"And the snows," went on Miguel unabashed, quoting a favourite couplet, "would not fall on your brow, Lola; why should we stop, they say, where the ground is whiter than we are?".

"*Anda!* (Go to!) Talk of other things."

"And the roses complain· that your lips are too red; and so do the flowers of the pomegranate also.

"A blushing face is better than a black heart."

"And your eyes are bright and sharp as daggers; they will do more mischief than all the Albacete knives in the Fair."

"*Calla!* (Shut up!) Don't talk me over and all my points as if I were a horse."

"*Prima*," said Miguel, quoting another couplet—

'A tall pine ; I cut it down.
An aloe ; I take out its sting.
A fierce bull ; I tame it—
But I cannot you.' "

" You are right, Miguel. I answer you that,
and at once in your own way—

'Si coronado vinieras
Como El Santo Rey David,
Y que a mis piés pusieras
No ha de cobrar el si.'

Were you to come crowned like King David,
to kneel at my feet, you should never gain
the 'yes' from me."

"You are thinking of that English officer,
Lola mia."

"Not I. I never saw him. I know him
not. Yet it was good of him to come to my
help."

" I would have carried you too, Lola mia,
but that he stepped before "——

"Could you lift me from the ground, think
you ? "

"Will you let me try ? "

"You had your chance. Chances are like
fruit. They don't grow twice, and you must

pick them when you can. But tell me, Miguelito, this English officer, was he handsome ? tall, *guapo, buen mozo ?* Would that I might see him·once, only once ! "

" Then have your wish, *prima.* Yonder he stands among the crowd outside."

" Which is he, cousin of my soul ? "

" He with the dust-coloured coat and *faja* (sash). Are not these English reckless in their dress ? Do they not go in clothes more shabby than a beggar's rags ? "

But Lola was at the moment indisposed to answer the question, for Frank had caught her eye, and had raised his hat in salutation, seeming thus to express his pleasure at seeing her so far recovered as to be present at the ball.

Lola coloured and bent her head slightly in return. Then without noticing Miguel's disparaging remarks on Frank's personal appearance, she cried to him—

" *Anda*, Miguelito, go and ask him to come in and join us."

" And why ? That I may be left out in · the cold ? That you may dance with him for the

rest of the night ?   No, *por mi salud*, by my
salvation, let him stay outside ! "

" You're afraid to talk English to him,
Miguel ; that's how the water runs. So much
for all your boastful talk of what you learnt
at school. English ! you cannot speak three
words."

" If I don't know English ! ask "——

" Prove it then."

Ridicule overcame jealousy, and Miguel,
pushing his way through the people, thus
addressed Frank Wriottesley——

" Mr English, good-bye.   Do you like to
enter ? Will you give yourself the pleasure
to walk by here ?   We stand diverting ourselves, and all within is at your disposition.
May you live for many years ! "

Frank smiled his thanks, and bowing, followed Miguel at once into the room.   He
had now the *entrée*, which was all he needed.
Presuming on the service he had rendered
Lola as an introduction, he went up to her,
saying—

" May I have the pleasure ? "——

" Me no spik English," said Lola, in a

faltering voice, blushing a rosy red; but she could not pretend to misunderstand him, just as she could not resist his invitation to dance.

The music—an old fiddle and a concertina, in the hands of two wandering Italian minstrels—was playing a galop, and in another moment Lola was, for the first time in her life, experiencing the pleasure of the poetry of very rapid motion. She had danced before this, with the school-girls at the convent; as a child, too, in the slow, graceful movements of a national dance, among the peasant people of the mountain towns; and with Miguel, that same night, she had tried a polka and a decorous waltz or two.

What we call "fast" dances are not thoroughly appreciated in Spain, except, perhaps, in Madrid, the court and capital; and even here, an English filly, fresh from school or in her first season, could, in racing metaphor, give the best blue-blooded belle any weight and still beat her head off.

All Lola's experiences and all her dreams came up to nothing like this. Round and round, faster and faster, till her feet barely touched the ground, and she seemed to be flying through the room in her partner's arms. How long it lasted, what tune they played, what Frank said to her—all was a blank, till the last moment when with a little sigh of pleasure, the pretty " o—e " that drops like a pearl from a Spanish girl's lips, she sank back into a seat crying, " *Yo no sé bailar* " —I know not how to dance.

For the rest of that evening Frank Wriottesley never left her side. They danced together again and again, till Miguel grew red with jealousy and rage. He would have appealed to his mother for protection, but Doña Teresa had not remained at the ball, and there was no authority present that Lola regarded in the least. Ramona enjoyed the fun, and encouraged her with many a nod and meaning wave of the fan, wishing that she could find for herself another devoted English officer, to pay her similar court.

A flirtation may be carried far even in a few hours, and without the possession of a language in common. The eyes can be made to talk far more expressively than the tongue,

and without the painful aid of grammar and
declensions. Frank spoke, unintelligibly, in
English, but then he laughed his own cheery,
bright laugh, and looked admiringly at Lola ;
and then Lola laughed too, replying in
Spanish, but turning upon him her beautiful
eyes, those large, soft, dreamy eyes, one flash
from which was worth a king's ransom.

And thus their acquaintance began ; and
when they parted for the night, it was with a
strong desire—not less eager in one than
the other—that they might meet again, and
soon.

CHAPTER V.

THE SPROULES.

FRANK thought a good deal of his adventure at San Roque next morning when he rode back to Gibraltar.

There was a cloud upon the Rock—the Levanter's nightcap—beneath which the town loomed black and gloomy, in marked contrast to the pleasant sunshine upon the scenes he was leaving behind. He had an engagement, too, to lunch at the Sproules, and although these had hitherto been his chief allies in the regiment, he could not conceal from himself a fear that to-day he was bound to be bored by them.

When the east wind blows at Gibraltar, you might buy all the inhabitants, men, women, and children, for a song. This wind—the Levanter—arrives surcharged with moisture, which it deposits on the summit of the Rock in the shape of a dense, dark cloud like an extinguisher. There is neither sun nor sky then, nor happiness for those who are in the town beneath; the streets are wet with rain that no one sees falling; every door bangs a dozen times an hour with the sudden gusts that sweep in curling eddies around the sloping sides of the great mountain-rock; life is almost at a stand-still. Some good souls have energy enough to pray forthwith for a change of wind, but to most in this terrible Levanter bare existence alone is possible. It depresses the spirits with a languor and prostration that is all its own. Without the slightest cause, children, English-born, howl dismally like woe-begone curs in the moonlight; strong men, with their shirts sticking to their backs, grow irritable, and sometimes swear; while the gentler sex pine away in peevish listlessness and *ennui*.

One of them, however, Janita Sproule,

as she sat near the door of the cottage to which fate and the Barrack Department had consigned her, was trying hard to fight against the influence of the weather. She sat bolt-upright in her chair, and fanned herself without ceasing; seeking thus to wrestle, both physically and mentally, with the atmosphere. Yet so far as outward looks went, she seemed fresh enough;—a small, trim person, her slight figure clad in the neatest of stone-grey dresses, with the whitest of cuffs and collar; rather a colourless woman, altogether pale in tone; the hair little deeper than flaxen, with just a shimmer of gold on each yellow tress, and her eyes, though good, of a cold china-blue.

"I look horribly washed out and faded," Mrs Sproule had said when she last consulted her glass, just an hour before. "This is the most detestable climate in the world, I think. And Mr Wriottesley is coming to lunch—I wish to goodness he was not— I hate being seen in such a limp, feeble condition. I only wish I was back at Chilham—just for five minutes under the trees on the lawn."

Chilham Priory was the home from which Captain Sproule half-a-dozen years before had won her. She was the eldest of a large family of daughters; and her mother, on the rack lest all should hang fire, had lost no opportunity of reminding Janita that she must marry well and soon. " It all depends how you play your cards," were the worldly-minded old woman's words. "With your natural advantages you ought to ʻdo well, if you are only decently careful." The *ménage* at the Priory was conducted on principles of the strictest economy. Bare necessaries of life were all that the stern father doled out to his family, and these were generally accompanied by gloomy references to gaol and the sheriff's officers. But they kept a saddle-horse for Janita, and made a show, before any possible suitor, of hospitality far above their means. With all this, Janita was not successful. She was already five-and-twenty, and no one had made her an offer yet. Frances, still in

the school-room, though long past the age
for coming out, was clamorous to begin her
campaign, and she was prettier than Janita.
Just then while on a visit to a neighbouring
garrison-town, Janita galloped straight into
the affections of Anthony Sproule, taking
his fancy as she would a fence, and forcing
him to marry her out-of-hand. Perhaps
Captain Sproule expected something handsome with a girl who was always so well
mounted. But in this he was disappointed.
She brought him nothing but her wits. Yet
the marriage was not an unhappy one.
Janita fell in readily with her husband's
ways, encouraging him in his sporting tastes,
and helping him often by her advice and
judgment. More than once she had squared
his betting-book, and had shown him a clean
road out of a bad business. Sproule could
look upon her as a partner in more ways
than one. Then she was a good manager;
the house was comfortable; she was sweet
and clean to look upon; could keep a secret,
and talk well upon the subjects Sproule
had most at heart; and as they had no

children, he found himself really better off after than before his marriage with Janita Helsham.

When Frank Wriottesley first joined the Halberdiers, the Sproules had been as kind to him as lay in their power. He came from Eton and Oxford with something of a reputation; his allowance was evidently first-rate, and he meant to hunt. Sproule sold him a horse—not a bad one; and Mrs Sproule spoke highly of his seat and hands. Frances, still unmarried, was brought down to Weedon, and stayed some months with her sister, riding Frank's horses often, and using her eyes upon him with their utmost effect. But although Wriottesley was then in the first flush of youth, he was yet no fool. He did not need the broad chaff of the mess-room to see through Mrs Sproule's manœuvres. Frances Helsham was not to his taste either; her face wanted expression, and her figure was too large. Besides which he was entirely dependent on an uncle, Sir Hector Harrowby, whose displeasure he had no desire to brave for any girl he had yet seen. Thus,

for the few years that preceded the remo-
val of the regiment to Gibraltar, Frank had
continued heart-whole, and, though friendly
with the Sproules, not exactly intimate.

But at Gibraltar it was different. Here,
for the first time, he missed the pleasant
country-houses that had been open to him at
home. Liking society, he found now quite a
dearth of it. Almost the only friendly house
at which he could visit was that of the
Sproules, and he soon took up with them
greatly. They were hospitable and kind,
made him at home at the cottage, and both
seemed glad to see him always. Sproule had
been of much assistance to him in forming his
stable, for Frank was fond of horses, and
meant to keep a string of both racers and
hunters.

Nor in this matter was Madame's advice
to be despised. The dealers, Gayetano, An-
tonio, Juan Gil, Pedro Gomez, and the rest,
deferred a good deal to the judgment of the
Señora, who sat above in the garden like a
Court of Appeal, while her husband and
Frank in the road down below saw the

horses show off their paces, or felt them over from head to foot with all a veterinary's skill. But patched-up screws, with rickety legs and elephantine teeth, would not go down with Mrs Sproule. It was not enough to deck out their long tails with ribbons, or plait their manes, or throw them on their haunches by a sharp tug at the cruel Spanish bit. The rocking-horse canter, the ambling gait, the useless " passage " from side to side— all these were quite thrown away upon her. These dealers, trained themselves in a sharp school, confessed that the English Señora was more than their match; and perhaps in their private talk called her a *chalan*, a cunning old fox of a horse-coper herself. But Frank Wriottesley benefited by all this, and so was drawn often enough to the Garden of Eden, as custom had quaintly christened the Sproules' picturesque home.

Now, Janita Sproule sat at the door of her cottage, a small place of three rooms only, all on the ground-floor, but with a verandah which was part and parcel of the house; and a garden, that might have been

included with the rest of the premises under
the general roof afforded to the whole
by the broad leaves and mighty branches
of the gigantic *bella sombra* tree behind.   It
was late in the season for flowers, but one
grand Bougainvillia was plastered against the
white walls—a mass still of big, beautiful
deep-blue blossoms; and passion-flowers hung
lovingly from the trellis-work above the door,
leaning forward as it were to enter as joint
owners and occupiers of the house.

"Mr Wriottesley!" said Mrs Sproule.
"Come in.   I was afraid it was some horrid
visitors, and not you."

"I am glad I am not included among the
'horrid.'"

"You know I look upon you quite as one
of ourselves."

"A *pal*, in fact."

"Well," said Mrs Sproule laughing, "if I
used words of that sort, I'd say *pal*.   But you
know what I mean.   Have you come to lunch?"

"Of course.   You asked me."

"Not that there's much.   Tough ration-
beef, or mutton, rather worse."

" The mutton here is goat. They only roll it from the signal-station down the face of the Rock to make it tender."

" The treatment is not very successful then. They'd better roll it up again. But there is nothing fit to eat in this place. Do you know, Mr Wriottesley, I begin to think Gibraltar is all a mistake."

" No place can be a mistake where you get such fruit as this," said Frank, producing a big basket or bag of wicker-work, which he had bought and filled as he passed through the market-place. It contained figs, purple and green, bursting with ripeness; grapes, muscatels, tender in tone as arsenical green; gorgeous melons from Valencia, having a fragrance all their own.

" The fruit is passable. I admit that," said Mrs Sproule. " But these figs should be iced. Did you ever eat iced figs ? No ? Then you don't know what their real flavour is. But there is no ice here," she went on.

" There was plenty yesterday."

" The admiral, before he went to sea this morning with the fleet, cleared out every ounce

of ice in the town. It's too bad, I declare ;
what is life without ice this weather ? "

" You look cool enough, Mrs Sproule."

" H—m ! I can't ice claret by looking at
it, or the sherry you will complain of by and
by at lunch."

" Sproule would be a lucky fellow if you
could. You would act as a refrigerator."

" With the bottles hung round me like a
necklace, I suppose !"

" But where is Tony ? "

Tony was Captain Sproule's family name.

" Why, I thought he was with you ! He
went down to barracks to join you after
breakfast."

" I've been away. I slept at San Roque
last night."

" And what took you there ? "

Mrs Sproule looked upon Frank Wriottesley
rather as her own property by this time, her
own special attendant ; and she wished to be
au fait with all he said or did.

" Business," replied Frank mysteriously.

" I give it up," said Mrs Sproule after a
pause. She was inclined to be snappish.

"I don't care to drag information out of people like teeth. It's too hot, besides, to be inquisitive."

"I went to the bull-fight, to be sure."

Frank reserved all mention of his meeting with Lola.

"And yesterday was Sunday! Oh, you bold, bad man!"

"Who is a bold, bad man?" asked another voice; adding, "We're all miserable sinners, though, and I am the chiefest of the gang. Here's Hop-i'-my-thumb gone back in 'the betting for the Goodwood Cup, and I stand to lose a cracker on the race."

"Another complaint against your beautiful Rock," said Mrs Sproule. "If you hadn't been so far off you might have got out of some of your money."

"You're right, my precious!—you always are. I could lay it off fast enough if I were within reach of the village."

This was Tony Sproule. In appearance he was like his talk. He ought to have been a jockey. It was all a mistake that he came of decent parents, and had been educated like a gentleman. The Heath at Ascot or Newmarket should have been his early home, where, a stray waif floating on the surface of its rascality, he would have found himself washed ashore some day against a training-stable, there to cling like a shell-fish or snail. There was something limpet-like in the lightness and tenacity with which he clung to his native home—the saddle. He had a small, good figure, though his shoulders were too high and his legs too thin; but his face was unpleasant. The small black eyes were restless and wandering; and when he humped his back and drew himself back to look at you evilly from under his bushy eyebrows, he was not unlike some nasty insect ready to make a sudden spring at your throat.

"Well, but tell us about the bull-fight," said Mrs Sproule; and Frank's thrilling description set her all agog to see one too.

" There's another to-day."

"I don't think you will like it, Mrs Sproule."

Frank did not want the Sproules at San Roque. He wished to return there himself,

but alone, to prosecute his acquaintance with
Lola.

But the more he threw cold water on the
scheme, the more anxious Mrs Sproule became. "What was she to ride?" asked her
husband, meaningly; and Frank could do no
less than place anything in his stable at her
disposal. So it came to pass, that within an
hour or two they were galloping, all three of
them, along the beach to San Roque.

If there had ever been a time when Frank
found a pleasure in Mrs Sproule's society, it
was now a thing of the past. That day, as
he cantered by her side, he thought her more
than uninteresting. The *petits soins* she demanded, and which at another time he might
have been disposed to render, were nothing less
than a positive nuisance now. At the Fair,
she insisted upon being escorted from booth
to booth, narrowly inspecting every shopman's stock-in-trade; while all the time Frank
was burning to get away in search of Lola.
Mrs Sproule took it for granted that her
cavalier was both ready and able to make
bargains for her, and kept on repeating, "Ask

him (the shopman) if he won't take less for
this," or, " Tell him I can get better any day
in London for next to nothing ;" till Frank
was quite wild, and finding it impossible to
interpret, lapsed at once into one-worded
sentences, such as—" *Mucho !* "   " *Cuanto !* "
" *No bono !* " which are the first simple utter-
ances of an Englishman in Spain.

"What has come over you, Mr Wriottesley ? " asked Mrs Sproule; " you look
bored to death.   Is there anything on your
mind ? "

"He is in love," Sproule broke in, "with
some of-these Spanish beauties."

" Nasty, black-skinned things ! " said the
English lady.   " I hope you have more taste."

A woman who is fair and pale-haired feels
it rather an insult when men openly admire
dark beauties.

"With their great staring eyes," she added,
as if to clench the argument, "and coarse
hair.   I don't expect they wash either."

Each little dig might have been intended
to enhance her own good points.   Her hair
was soft and silky, her eyes quiet and unob-

trusive; and in her habit of white piqué, fresh from the wash, she looked as spick and span as a new pin.

"There mayn't be as many bath-tubs about as there are in barracks," protested Frank; "but it's not fair to call them dirty. Look what clean linen they wear."

White shirts and petticoats, scrupulously got up, are the rage with Spaniards, male and female. The peasant women and the lowest labourers sport linen, on great occasions, as white as snow. The beds in the inns may be furnished with many unpleasant lodgers, but the sheets will be white and clean, and the pillowcases have an edging of white lace. A tablecloth and a napkin, coarse but clean, are provided at every meal, even in a hovel.

"I'll make you a present of your friends. I won't say another word against them or their ways, if you promise to be in a better humour."

But Frank continued *distrait*. His eyes were wandering to and fro among the crowd, restlessly seeking the face of his new friend. When the time for the bull-fight approached,

he tried hard to escape going, but Mrs
Sproule had set her heart upon it.

"You won't be able to stand it—indeed
you won't," he said.

"I should just like to see the commence-
ment."

"No lady—at least no English lady—ought
to go."

"Thank you, Mr Wriottesley; but I am
perfectly well able to decide upon such a
point for myself."

Mrs Sproule was getting a little angry
with her friend Frank. He was generally
so ready to enter at once into her views.
To-day he was disagreeable and contuma-
cious.

"Besides," she added, "my husband does
not object. What more need be said?"

"Sproule knows nothing about it. He
has not seen the thing as I did yesterday.
It's quite horrible. And you pretend to be
devoted to horses, Mrs Sproule!"

"I am fonder still of having my own way.
And now, by persuading me not to go in,
you only make me all the more anxious."

" If she's got her head, you must let her bolt her own way," remarked Sproule.

" Come, Mr Wriottesley ; don't let us quarrel over it. You'll go with us."

" My accompanying you is not indispensable, I suppose ? You meant to go whether I join or not ? "

" Most certainly. Your escort is not in the least necessary. My husband is here, thank you. He will see me through it."

" Not through all of it. But if you will excuse me, I had much rather remain outside."

Mrs Sproule tossed her head, as much as to say he might do what he pleased, and then gathering up the skirts of her habit went off with her husband.

Frank, left to himself, took post at the entrance of the Alameda, and watched all day. But no Lola was to be seen. By the time he again met the Sproules, his temper was worse than ever. As he had prophesied, Mrs Sproule had been unable to endure the spectacle. She came out after the first charge, and confessed that Frank had been right.

"I wish I had taken your advice," she said, turning very pale. "I should like now to go straight home."

"I'm your man, my precious!" cried Sproule. "It's monstrous slow here, and I've not seen a decent horse in the Fair."

"Will you come, Mr Wriottesley? Don't let us drag you back sooner than you had intended;" adding, with something of a sneer, "Doubtless there are attractions for you in this place."

Frank preferred to stay, of course; so his friends rode back without him, and he turned towards the Alameda once more. Again it was crowded, and as evening drew on there was the same assemblage at the Casino as on the previous night. Frank, taking it for granted he would be welcome, walked in. Miguel was one of the first persons he met, and from him he inquired for the ladies.

"My parent Lolita" (he was speaking of his cousin and our heroine, but he was also translating literally from his own idiom) 'has gone to Gibraltar back. Don Mariano, her grandfather, has put himself too choleric, more rabid than a black bull."

It was too true. An imperious mandate had come early on Monday morning to San Roque, desiring Lola and her dueña to return forthwith to Gibraltar. Don Mariano had waited patiently on Sunday evening for their return, till the gun fired at nine, and then he knew that they must now be on the wrong side of the closed gates of the fortress. There they must remain outside till morning ; and he cursed Josefa loudly for her carelessness, taking for granted that she was chiefly to blame. Matters were not mended much when Josefa's messenger turned up at the cottage, smelling strongly of aguardiente, and with but a confused recollection of his instructions. All that he remembered distinctly was the accident in the bull-ring, and the gossip that had gone about of the wounded *picador* being Josefa's son. This he told Mariano ; but added no word of the cousins with whom Lola was to stay the night. Josefa's excuse for remaining absent was thus unspoken, and in its absence old Bellota grew furious. He would discharge

Josefa at once from her situation, would drive her forth from the garrison, and brand her as a lying, disreputable, untrustworthy harridan.

But he did not forget to recall them to the Rock. In obedience to this order, Lola and her dueña, the latter trembling, the former pouting and discontented, took to their *calesa* about mid-day, and were conveyed back just as the stream of sight-seers was bound once more San Roque-wards. Among others who crowded and jostled them, they passed Frank Wriottesley riding with Mrs Sproule.

Poor Lola! This was her devoted admirer of the night before, who had looked so long and lovingly into her eyes, and who had gone so far to win her affections. And yet within a few hours he must have forgotten her altogether. Why else was he leaning over in his saddle and talking thus earnestly to this fair-haired Englishwoman? She was *rubia* (yellow), and so was he. Naturally this was his *gusto*, his taste, a countrywoman of his own rather than a black, gipsy-faced Southerner who knew no English ways and but few English words.

She was too young and too simple to be able to conceal her chagrin from Josefa. The wily dueña had heard something of what had happened, and seeing Lola colour as Frank rode by, guessed directly that it was he who had assisted her the day before.

" That *rubio*, that light-haired Englishman, do you know him, *hija?* " asked Josefa.

"Which? There are many passing."

" Am I blind, Dolorcita *mia?* are my eyes choked up like grass upon a sand-hill? I mean that tall one who rode with the English lady in the white habit."

Lola hung her head.

" Am I to tell the *señor amo* that you have made this friend? *Pues*, indeed, that was all that was needed; he will now be wild indeed."

" No, no, *querida* Josefiya; good, kind, dear Josefa; say nothing to him of this," cried Lola, leaning her head against the old woman's shoulder.

" How then? you have found a *novio* (a lover)? "

" A lover ! I hate him."

For Lola had now learnt for the first time
the meaning of jealousy. And Josefa had her
secret, to be used or not, later, just as that
astute schemer considered likely to prove
most to her own advantage.

CHAPTER VI.

"SWEETWATER FARM."

"THOU marchest—this day, this hour," cried old Bellota sternly, as the dueña entered the house with her charge.

There was a steep ascent up the garden walk from the road outside, and Josefa, being short-winded, was at first quite defenceless. She knew she was in for a battle royal—what is called in Spanish a "St Quentin's day."

"Hadst no shame?" went on her master, "no shame? Thou bold, brazen woman, that I picked up from a gutter! From the fish filth in your own foul and poisonous home! *Thou* to take charge of the star of my life, of my sole and only joy; this priceless pearl, this great and rare jewel—my Lolita! Thou! *Canalla*, brigand, ostrich, *tarasca* (serpent), vile,

shameless Jewess from Hottentot India! By
the soul of my mother, by the life of the god
Bacchus, by a thousand on horseback, it was
an evil day when you first darkened my
doors."

Josefa had thrown herself into a chair, and
was using her fan violently. Rage now con-
spired with fatigue to keep her silent; she
could as yet say nothing in her defence, and
Don Mariano's tirade ended in a long whine
of fury.

Lola took up the cudgels for her dueña.

"*Oye* (listen), *abuelito*. Don't put yourself
into a passion. What fly has stung you?"

"Be silent, child. Put not your spoon
into this stew. No one gave you a candle
to hold at this funeral. It is no business of
yours."

"Whose then? what more? Not my
business, indeed, when you have torn me
from San Roque just as the fun began, when
I was diverting myself enough to "——

"You should have come back last night.
But I blame you not, Dolorcita; you are
softer than a glove, sweeter than a stew of

apples. The fault was none of yours. But it belongs to this *picarona*, this great lump of evil, this Cain in cunning, this ugly witch, who must needs disobey my orders. And why? For a son she hardly knows; one who left her—no wonder either—as soon as he could walk. *Canario!* defend me from such a son. But as is the bell so is the clapper. He is of the same stick as the old tree. Apple-trees grow apples, and oyster-beds oysters, and a bad bough can only come from a rotten trunk. This one here," he cried, pointing disdainfully to Josefa, "is fit only for firewood. But I'll warm your soup; I'll make you eat hot garlic. I'm neither lame nor left-handed. To the old dog you must say more than *tus! tus!* Not another hour shalt thou continue under this roof. Great mountain of bad flesh, indecent Jezebel, why don't you speak? Am I to talk all day, throwing pearls before pigs, and you pointing your finger there like the clock of Pamplona, that points but never strikes?"

"Señor Don Mariano," replied Josefa at

length, with as much dignity as her passion would allow her to assume, "I am not a gun. I cannot go off pop; I must have time to speak."

"You shall have no longer time than is needed to pack your trunk and march. You can have no excuses that will gain my forgiveness."

"Then I need not say them. *En boca cerrada no entran moscas.* Flies do not enter the shut mouth. You have neither birth nor breeding. Your words are like feathers for the wind to fly away with. They have neither weight nor meaning. I will not answer them. I am an honest woman ; and I have but one son"——

"Of whom you may well be proud— proud as is the hen of her addled egg. A good-for-nothing idler, a *gaznapiro.* Like a bat—neither bird nor rat. One who ran away"——

"Other people's children have run away before now, good señor," said Josefa slowly and with meaning.

Don Mariano understood her, and instantly

became quite livid with passion. He could not speak; his fury both blinded and made him dumb; but he rushed at Josefa with upraised hand, as if to strike her.

"For shame, grandfather!" said Lola, quietly interposing; "you will be sorry afterwards. What has she said?"

And then it seemed to occur to Bellota that he was going too far. Possibly the desire to prevent further disclosures from Josefa—for Lola had been kept in ignorance always of the causes which had led to her mother's death—checked him more effectually than his granddaughter's remonstrance. But the look that he gave Josefa told her she had offended him so deeply that she might expect but little mercy at his hands.

"*Fuera!* Be off! Get out!" said the old man in a hoarse voice, and then dropped exhausted into a seat, while Josefa slank away.

Lola had never seen him thus excited before. Brought up at a distance from him, their meetings had been marked always by soft caresses and an almost doating fondness. She had no notion that far down in the

depths of his nature there smouldered these
fiery passions, these strong emotions, which
Bellota owed not alone to his Southern blood,
but also to the grievous sorrows that had
shadowed his early life. Lola would have
forgiven her grandfather readily enough had
she guessed at the causes which had thus
roused his rage like a whirlwind. But as a
whirlwind it had arisen suddenly, and as
such it suddenly sank and died away. His
first thought was for the child of his heart,
who had stood the while watching him,
anxious, and not a little perturbed in spirit
at the new phase just revealed to her of her
grandfather's character.

He guessed in a measure what was passing
through her mind, for his next words were
those of apology and regret.

"Forgive me, darling of my life! It is
not often that the black blood is stirred, but
when I am touched here," he said, pointing to
his heart, "I am Mariano Bellota no more.
It is the accursed fiend himself that speaks, and
his very spirit that prompts me. I should
have killed her then had a knife been handy."

"But why, *abuelito?* She said little to vex you. Why so angry?"

"No matter. It is past." Mariano did not wish to give rise to suspicions in his granddaughter's mind. "Tell me what became of you, *Lolita de mi alma,* when this harpy went to nurse her boy? What friends did you meet with to shelter and take care of you? or did she—may the curse of Columbus consume her—carry you with her to the hospital?"

"*Nada.* Of course not. I was with ·my cousins."

"Your cousins!" exclaimed Don Mariano, surprised. This was the first he had heard of the relations from Ximena. "And which, pray?"

"Doña Teresa from Agua Dulce, and Ramona and Miguel."

"Did you meet them at the Fair?"

"If I met them at the Fair! *Abuelo! estas tonto?* Are you not sane? Clearly we met them at the Fair. Did not Josefa herself send you word that Doña Teresa and the others had come to San Roque?"

"Then it is this *malvado*, this worthless Matias Curro, who has made all the mischief. When he came last night as drunk as a rickety wheel, he said no word about his cousins. He told me Josefa had found her son, a *picador*, at the fight, and that she had stayed to nurse him, as he was wounded by a bull."

Perhaps Don Mariano began to be a little sorry for his hastiness. But he was not yet disposed to forgive Josefa for what she had said.

"I am glad you met them, Dolorcita,— these cousins. And you enjoyed yourself?"

"Pretty well."

"And the bulls? *Qué tal?* What were they like?"

"Don't talk of the fight, *abuelo. Santissima Virgen!* It makes me sick to think of it. When Pepe, poor lad, was wounded, I fainted, and they had to carry me away."

Lola did not care to mention how she had been removed from the ring.

"Little children should not go to such spectacles. They are meant for stronger stomachs."

"It was foolish of me to faint, but the sight of the blood, and the poor horses, and Pepe almost killed—how could I help it?"

"And you were very bad, light of my eyes?" inquired the old grandfather very anxiously.

"Aunt Teresa took me to her house, and I soon got well—so well, that in the evening I went to the Casino ball."

"And you danced?"

"All night, *abuelito*; it was like heaven."

"With Miguel?"

"And with others," added Lola, feeling compelled to pay a slight passing tribute to truth.

"Shall we not know the beginning of your loves, Dolorcita? or does love like secrecy, as do the nightingales the dark?"

"Ay, *abuelo*; love is like the orange, not always sweet—there is something bitter in it too at times."

"So sad and you beginning life, when hope is still quite fresh and green! Know you not the saying 'of love and soup, the first helping is the best?'"

"Love is like the mosquito, grandfather;
it stings, raises a sore, and goes away sing-
ing."

"Hast felt the wound already, child? Was
there a *pollo* (a lad) among them all who
would not hold you dearer than holy water
if he got the chance? You were too proud
to them; I'll wager my nose on it."

"The man who wants me must come after
me," said Lola rather sadly, thinking of
Frank's supposed defection. "The rivers
run down to seek the sea, and so must they
do who would wish to win my love. But
Josefa?"

"She goes. I cannot admit such conduct.
Her tongue is longer than an alcalde's wand
of office."

Lola was tender-hearted, and she liked
Josefa. Besides, the dueña had her secret,
and it was well to keep good friends.

"She will not offend you thus again. And
her sin—what was it? She is a mother, and
could not leave her son to die."

"What know you of such feelings?"

"My heart tells me. Would you desert

your child, *abuelo*, neglected, to die alone, without one loving word or friendly hand?"

"Well, well; we will see."

"That's what the blind man said, but he did not see for all that."

"Artful! you have more talk than an attorney to gain your ends."

"She stays?"

"If you wish it, yes. But let her keep from my sight, or I may do her some mischief yet."

Nor did Lola's advocacy end here. Knowing that Josefa's heart was just now bound up in the welfare of the son in hospital, she gained her grandfather's permission for the dueña to remain at San Roque till Pepe was convalescent. Don Mariano consented to this with a bad grace, and only after Lola had agreed to spend the interval at Ximena with her cousins. She could not be left alone at Rosia Cottage, he said, and this was the only alternative. To this Lola could make no valid objections. After all, it suited her purpose to retire for a time to the *Cortijo*. Before starting, however, she one day asked her grand-

father, somewhat abruptly, whether he could
ride on horseback.

" *Caramba !* of course."

" Is it difficult ? "

" Not for young bones, before the pains
and tortures of old age commence. But
what——do you wish to ride too ? So you
shall, *querida*, but upon a *jamuga*, a pack-
saddle with a chair and straps to keep you
from falling."

" *Anda !* Throw that bone to some other
dog. Have I not ridden thus for years, at a
foot's pace and upon the back of a patient
mule ? . No, grandfather ; my desire is to
mount a pure-bred Cordoves, a steed of fire,
of lineage, and race, to wear an amazona, and
sit sideways like an English lady."

" You would be terrified out of your small
wits."

" English ladies are not."

" They learn it young. That which is
learnt in the cradle lasts all one's life."

" I am no coward. What others do, I can
accomplish also."

" Saddle the water-boy's donkey then, *Lolita*

mia. It's better to be carried peacefully by an ass than kicked off by a horse."

But Lola, as usual, had her own way. She started within a few days for Ximena, convoyed thither by Josefa, who returned next day to San Roque. Part of Lola's baggage was a second-hand side-saddle, which old Bellota had rummaged out of one of his stores. He sent word, also, to Lucas, the eldest son and managing man upon the farm, that a horse—a gentle, well-bred, lady's horse—was to be found at a moderate price, and that Lola was to be taught, if possible, to ride.

Why had this sudden fancy seized the girl? For no reason but that she might do as the English did; that she might, by some effort of her own, bridge over the gulf that seemed to separate her from Frank Wriottesley. All the English ladies rode on horseback; this much Lola thought she might also acquire, if she were unable to change her spots, to whiten her clear olive skin, and give another tinge to her lustrous purple hair—though these were not impossible feats either, had she been a little more conversant with the advantages of civilisation.

Sweetwater Farm, the Cortijo de Agua Dulce, the home of Lola's cousins, lay a mile or two from the town of Ximena, and some half-dozen leagues from Gibraltar. To reach it, you passed through the whole length of the great cork-wood, by a track, nothing more; and leaving the "Long Stables" on the left, opened out upon a wide plain, which extended to the very base of the hill on which Ximena stands. Most of the towns in Southern Andalucia are perched thus, like an eagle's eyrie on the top of a tall peak. They were built so for safety, when Moorish or Christian foragers harried the lands around.

The herds you passed in this plain belonged mostly to Sweetwater Farm, where more business was done in raising stock than in mere husbandry. For the latter, a few fields of barley and beans and an olive grove sufficed, with several acres of vines, from which they got wine sufficient for their home consumption. The wealth at Agua Dulce was in cattle, in droves of small, wiry oxen with tremendous

horns, that lolled most of the summer days
in the half-dry pools of the shallow river, or
followed the tinkling bells of their leaders
from pasture to pasture; in troops of brood
mares with their attendant colts; in pigs,
strong, little, black brutes, more like wild
boars, whose flesh, acorn-fed, was to be
turned by and by into sweet hams and good,
juicy bacon. Last of all, in bulls—in big,
fierce *toros*, bred for the national amphitheatre
with consummate pains and infinite tests to
prove their courage, endurance, and animal
strength. These last were herded apart from
the possible intrusion of irritating strangers,
in spots more retired; ranging there alone
with their especial herdsmen and their companions, the *cabestros*, or tame oxen, whom
they loved and trusted, only to be some day,
Judas-like, by them betrayed.

Matters were carried on in a very primitive fashion at Agua Dulce. The common
appliances of English farmers were still
unknown in this secluded corner of a
backward country. Steam ploughs, patent
thrashing-machines, wire-fencing, and chemical

manures had never hope for trial there.
That which their ancestors had worked
with was good enough for them—the clumsy
plough, drawn at a snail's-pace by patient
oxen, the water raised by a *noria* or Moorish
millwheel, the corn trampled out by the hoofs
of horses. What did they want with fences?
The mountains themselves served as barriers
to the plains; and right up to their base
the cattle might wander at will. Manures,
patent or other, were superfluous where,
under the bright sun of the South, the
fertile soil teemed with richness and multi-
plied fifty-fold.

The *cortijo* itself was a big rambling place,
capable of standing a siege. It was quite
self-contained, within high walls—a small
colony or fortress independent of external
assistance, having granaries and storerooms,
forge, bakehouse, kitchen, all inside. The
stables would have held a troop of cavalry,
for which the yard or *corral* was a spacious
exercising ground; in the large *huerta* or
orchard grew fruit-trees in abundance, in
the small home garden vegetables and any

quantity of herbs suitable for medicinal pur-
poses—an important item of produce, seeing
that with concoctions of various plants Doña
Teresa doctored everybody within miles. As
for the house, it was roomy, bare, and rather
comfortless. There was a second story, but
the family from choice inhabited the ground-
floor, in which the rooms stood almost
without furniture beyond a walnut-wood
cupboard here and there, a few high-backed
chairs with rush bottoms; for carpet, a few
large circular mats of *esparto* grass; and
for decoration, one or two framed oil-pictures
—bad imitations of Murillo, Zurbaran, and
Ribera, all of which were nevertheless
chained to the walls lest in some new
invasion they might be stolen, like others
in the old days, and removed to France.

The chief personage at the farm was
Doña Teresa Panfila Peñaflor, to whom we
have already been introduced, a wizened,
leathery-faced old dame, not really old,
being barely fifty; but people age prema-
turely in a land which turns lakes into
salt-pans and makes raisins from juicy grapes.

Her voice, sweet perhaps when her husband courted her, was sour now as an unripe pomegranate pip; and her manner was always imperious, as became the representative of several illustrious families—a *hidalga*, the daughter of some one, with ancestors, many of them distinguished, of whom she was continually speaking, and coats of arms enough to furnish a stock-in-trade for half-a-dozen colleges of heralds. She was pious to a fault—in other words, bigoted, narrow-minded, and superstitious. Day and night there burnt a small lantern in a niche near the main entrance, which was tended by her own hand, and dedicated to the patron saint of her deceased spouse. It gave her some concern that her eldest son, Lucas, who was the real, but not the nominal master of the farm, belonged to the more advanced school of politics, and counted it part of his creed to despise openly the religion of his forefathers, expressing the most vigorous contempt for the priests and their ceremonies, characterising them as *cosas de mujeres*, things fit only for women.

This Lucas was of a type occasionally to be met with among the upper class of country folk in Southern Spain. Coarse in mind and in manner, unless he saw some advantage was to be gained by being gracious, a swaggerer and a bully, at home or in the immediate neighbourhood everybody deferred to Lucas Peñaflor, and when he opened his lips, no dog presumed to bark. He already lorded it over all the people of the farm as if it were his own property, whereas his mother had still a life-interest in it, and Lucas was only her overseer and managing man. The place was prosperous, yet the Peñaflors were by no means rich, and all alike had to work, except Alejandro, the second son, who was a lieutenant in a line regiment, and generally away from home. Miguel, the younger brother, was clerk and steward of accounts, a sort of slave to Lucas, who made his life a burthen to him. Miguel was small, and not courageous, and he thought it better to endure in silence the tyranny of his elder brother. Ramona, the only sister, shared with her mother 'the duties of the house, not disdaining at times to take her place at the washing-boards by the river-side, and assisting in the kitchen, or in the various operations for salting and curing bacon, preserving fruit at the proper seasons, cooking, clear-starching, and making herself generally useful. She had learnt from her mother to prepare a *gazpacho* (an oil-and-water salad), or to stew a fowl with green peppers, against any cook in Southern Spain.

CHAPTER VII.

UNDER MARTIAL LAW.

CHEERY, light-hearted Frank Wriottesley! The reader will hear much of him in these pages. He was in truth a very gallant young fellow, full of life and spirits, with a merry heart and a loud, ringing voice, that it did you good to hear. And such energy, such vitality, as there was in the man! He was never bored, never out of sorts, never at a loss to fill his vacant hours. Very keen in those field-sports to which he had been trained from his earliest youth, and in all of which he excelled; cunning, too, and clever with his fingers, ready to make you anything from a gun-case to a patent toothpick. In the by-season, when his hunting-coat and tops were laid on one side, and his gun lay idle, he found employment at his lathe, and littered all his barrack-room with chips and shavings. A great contriver was Frank, and fashioner of raw material. Nothing pleased him half so much as to be asked to devise something new—a new bit, or a new knife, or a new plan of tying up Mrs Sproule's skirts, to keep them from trailing in the mud. He was no great lover of books, although he had a well-thumbed copy of " Hawker," another of " Hutchinson on Dog-breaking," and knew most of " Youatt on the Horse" by heart. But, as a general rule, having such a super-abundance of animal spirits, he had not the patience to sit still and read. He wanted to be up and doing always. Of an evening, when his day's work was finished—a long day's work, self-chosen—he wanted to go to bed, so as to be up with the lark and begin again. So he could not afford the time for study, even if he had had the incli-nation. But though no bookworm, Frank had " parts," which he could exhibit if put to the push, only his nature was foreign to sedentary employment. He was essentially a man of action—one who spoke fast, and was generally in a hurry; a blithe, eager, impetuous youth, who would have had strong likes and dislikes, were he not too good-natured to hate even an enemy long. Nevertheless, this same softness of heart gave promise that, when the occasion came for him to fall in love, his passion would be too ardent and overpowering to be checked by ordinary obstacles.

Frank's childhood had been spent with his father in Canada — in the far North-west, where for many years Colonel Wriottesley commanded an important detachment. The place, Fort Garry, is even now but little known; in the time of Frank's youth it might have been called the uttermost Thule of the earth. Here, amidst wild sports, and in a semi-savage state of existence, Frank was nurtured till the time came for him to go to school. His parents parted with him —their only child—with poignant sorrow; but the separation was so notably to Frank's advantage, that his mother could not refuse to let him go to England. They never saw

him again.   A year later, returning homeward
from Quebec, the steam-ship in which they
had taken passage was lost at sea.   Colonel
and Mrs Wriottesley were among those who
perished.

· The blow fell heavily upon Frank at Uppingham School, but it was with a thrill of
pride for all his grief that he read how gallantly his parents had met their death—how
conspicuous had been his father's efforts to
save life, and lessen confusion on board
the sinking ship—how nobly his mother had
sought to instil comfort, and preach resigna-
tion, to the terrified women who clung around
her in the last awful moments, when death
stared all in the face.   Both had refused to
leave the wreck till the last, and thus delay-
ing till it was too late, they went down with
the ship.   But they left to Frank a heritage of
heroism which, boy-like, he treasured far above
a more worldly and tangible inheritance.

The orphan boy, unhappily, needed more than
this to keep him alive and give him a fair
start in life.   In the matter of pounds, shillings,
and pence, he was left but poorly off, and he

might have found himself in dire distress had not help come whence he least expected it.

His nearest relative was a certain Sir Hector Harrowby, a baronet of good estate in Essex. Sir Hector for years past had been—like the Civil Service—thrown open to competition. A childless old bachelor, he made no secret of his desire to adopt any boy among his own relations that might suit his fancy. There was no lack of candidates, of course—sex and relationship were the only indispensable qualifications; but it mattered little to Sir Hector whether it was sister's son or fifteenth cousin many times removed. So long as the candidate owned some kinship, and was not a girl, Sir Hector was satisfied. A girl he would not have—he professed to hate the whole female race. Tradition said that, ages before, when he was no great match, a lady of rank, higher than his own, had jilted him. This of itself would explain his unreasoning dislike for the whole sex, but the dislike was more fancied than real. Down in the bottom of his heart he was faithful still to the memory of his first love. In that early venture had

been embarked all the wealth of his youthful
affections—embarked only to be shipwrecked,
though not utterly lost. Just as the blackened
ribs of a ship that is cast away stand long
superior to choking sand-drifts, or the cease-
less wash of waves, so the ruins of the
hull that had once carried all his hopes, de-
fied the forgetfulness of increasing years, and
the selfishness of riches. To the last her
image was fresh ˏand green in his mind; for
her sake he never married, missing thus that
which no money can purchase—the honest,
disinterested affection of his own-begotten
children.

But the tender place in Sir Hector's heart
was carefully covered over and concealed.
In the eyes of each new trembling aspirant
for his favours he was all but an ogre—a
tall terrible man impossible to please. He
towered with imposing figure above the
would-be heir—already carefully prepared by
home-preaching for this momentous ordeal—
and frightened him into fiddle-strings, long
before he spoke, by the hardness of his face
and the stern look in his dark penetrating

eyes. There was a great martinet lost in Sir Hector; he ought to have been an admiral or a general officer; and indeed it was a secret disappointment to him that his father in early life, before the title and family property had come to their branch, had sent him to the bar, instead of allowing him to enter either military or naval services. Sir Hector ruled his household with a rod of iron, calling for the most unhesitating obedience to his will. Everything in his house was in apple-pie order; the whole establishment went like clock-work. The servants were drilled in their duties from the day they joined, by the unyielding butler— no bad lieutenant to so severe a chief. Order, discipline, and punctuality reigned supreme at Grimswych Park.

When Frank came to England from Hudson's Bay, his father wrote to Sir Hector— his wife's brother—explaining that he was sending his boy to school, and that, exiled himself, he longed to find a friend for the child at home. But the appeal was lost upon Sir Hector. Just then a candidate was on

probation, who promised rather well. His
voice was good—one of the aspirant's first
duties was to read aloud to Sir Hector—
and he showed great aptitude with his gun.
It was not till the news of the shipwreck
appeared in the papers, with the account
published by the survivors of Colonel and
Mrs Wriottesley's conduct on board, that Sir
Hector bethought him of the lonely orphan
at Uppingham. There was no one in favour
at the moment—the last candidate had ruined
his fortunes by peppering the best pointer in
the coverts—and a mandate was forthwith
despatched summoning Frank to Grimswych
Park.

It had come to be rather a joke at the
little station where Sir Hector's guests alighted
to see the new heirs arrive—and soon afterwards depart.

" There was two here last week," the porter
would remind the stationmaster. " They
both on 'em stayed only an hour."

" Ah ! but that little chap as was brought
by his mother. She come back same fly.
Sir Hector don't have no petticoats up there,

he don't. But the young'un stayed—what? A month or more?"

"Keeper told me he peppered Ponto, and the Squire took on awful. And there was that stout lad"——

"Him as couldn't sit the kicking pony? ah! I mind him well," went on the station-master laughing.

"And here's another on 'em," was Frank's salutation as he jumped out of the railway carriage at Grimswych.

There was a mangy terrier dog at his heels, and he had a ferret in each pocket. Among his traps were a well-worn trout-rod and basket covered with fish scales, one or two pea-shooters, a bat, and in his hand one of those specially infernal machines called catapults, from which he at once discharged a well-aimed shot at the stationmaster's favourite hen.

A small Whitechapel pony-chaise was in waiting from the "Big House," as the Park was familiarly styled.

"Is that for me?" cried young Frank, vaulting nimbly over the station-railings. "All

right! Here! lay hold," he added, sharply
bundling all his miscellaneous belongings into
the groom's hands or on to his knees. "Bring
out my box, will you, old stupid! Don't
mind the rooster. Here's a bob—that'll buy
you another. Now, then, off you go—sharp's
the word;" and Frank was driven away in
triumph, leaving the railway officials amazed.

"He's not much like the rest," said the
porter thoughtfully. "There's some spunk in
him anyhow."

"He needn't have got knocking my fowls
about," remarked the stationmaster. "But
Sir Hector will bring him to his bearings
pretty fast, I make no doubt. He'll be here
again in a day or two—outward bound."

It was not long since Frank's great grief
had fallen upon him, but he was not made to
mope and moan. Besides, sorrow runs off
the young like water from a duck's back.
Frank was growing out of his fast, leaving it
behind, like the decent black trousers were
leaving already the neighbourhood of his
boots, and the black coat cuffs shrank back
from his strong red wrists. He had mourned

his parents well and truly, but by nature his temperament was buoyant and hopeful. He could not droop for long; he was more like a strong steel spring, that recovers itself with a quick sharp snap. And now we find him overflowing with spirits, keenly enjoying the new situation in which he found himself.

All along the road he sought for a bent, legitimate or the reverse, for his superabundant energies. His catapult was never idle; and as the trap passed rapidly through the village he saluted the bystanders with some very sharp file-firing. Then, after goading the pony to fresh efforts by raining pellets from his pea-shooter about the poor brute's ears, nothing would satisfy him but he must drive.

"Can you drive, sir?" asked the groom respectfully, but with an accent of strong doubt.

"Can I drive! Did you ever drive a team of ten? I have—dogs—five couple, one behind the other, and a whip that would crack like a pistol. I'm all right, bless you. I don't remember, man, when I hadn't reins in my hand."

He was all right with the reins; one of his earliest lessons had been to drive a sleigh with its accompaniment of merry tinkling bells. But the whip was too great a temptation for him. Not that the pony wanted it, but Frank wanted to use it. Before long they were flying along the road at a racing-pace, past the park-palings, through the lodge gates, up the avenue to the very hall-door.

"Was you a-driving, Smithers?" asked the very decorous butler who came to answer the bell. "I see'd the cart a-comin' along the drive, and I could a-hardly believed my eyes. Sir Hector don't like his horses bucketted, and the coachman'll have something to say to you before you're a much *h*older man."

"Don't blow him up, sir." Frank did not know to whom he was speaking; it might be Sir Hector himself, or some clerical friend of the family. "It was my fault; I haven't had the ribbons in my hands for a couple of years."

"I beg your pardon, sir," said Mr Butter-field with an air of some condescension. "Of course, if it was you, sir. Will you please to walk in, sir? I am Sir Hector's own man, sir. He desired me to show you into the library when you arrived. Johnson!" he added, to a passing footman, " Mr Wriottesley's things to the blue room, and get them unpacked. This way, sir," and then he ushered Frank across the entrance-hall to a snug room filled with books, which Sir Hector made his home.

" You'd best be quite still, sir," went on the butler in a patronising voice. " There's a many nick-nacks and jiggering-dandies about, and Sir Hector don't like nothing meddled nor muddled."

" All right, I don't mean to play foot-ball with the best china."

Frank's reverence was never very long-lived, and it had melted like snow in summer when he found that this pompous person was only a servant after all.

" No, sir, I suppose not," replied the butler gravely. He was being made fun of, and this was something new. Frank's predecessors had rather cultivated Sir Hector's confidential man, and Mr Butterfield was already prejudiced against Frank by his independence.

"Here is this day's *Times*, sir, and some new books as came last week ; but Sir Hector will not be long, I don't doubt. He only went to the Home Farm."

The day's *Times* was duly displayed . to Frank's indifferent eyes, and the butler vanished.

What did Frank care for the day's *Times?* He had not yet got to be interested in the money articles, nor in the "leaders," nor yet in the foreign intelligence. The agony column might have amused him, had he known where to look for it; but failing this, he found the newspaper but dry reading. So his eyes began to wander about, then he fidgetted in his chair. How could he sit still when there was so much to stare at in the room ? Books in the first place, and almost in any quantity : the master of Grimswych knew them to be better company often than living Christians. Then Sir Hector was a *dilettante* and an art collector, and the room was full of fine prints, good drawings, and articles of *vertu*—charming

chefs-d'œuvre from the best Italian chisels, ex-
quisite bronzes, wondrous ivory-work, and
richly-carved cabinets full of costly china.
Where the bookcases did not take up wall
space stood shelf upon shelf of specimens,
collections complete, entomological, ornitho-
logical, and so forth; for Sir Hector, among
other pursuits, dabbled in natural history.
It was these that attracted Frank most; and
the *vis inertiæ*, so to speak, of the butler's
caution having been once overcome, he wandered freely from point to point with all the
ardour of a young and inexperienced sightseer
let loose for the first time among an exhibition
of treasure.

In addition to those in the glass cases,
a number of stuffed birds stood on high,
crowning the book-shelves. They were too
big mostly to be on a lower level, and being
thus out of reach, they hung like forbidden
fruit, tempting Frank to climb up and pick
them. It is probable that he would have
resisted successfully had he not espied among
them a fine white-headed Erne—the American
eagle, a king among birds—which he had

seen once or twice before, and readily recognised now.

To move the library ladder and run up
the rungs was the matter of a moment.
Frank proposed to himself to bring the bird
down and examine it more closely.

He was at the top of the ladder, and had
seized his prey, when some one called to
him from the door—

"Well, well, upon my word, sir!"

Frank thought it was the butler returned,
and replied saucily—

"All right, old cock—right as ninepence."

"You had better come down—in point
of fact, you must come down." There was
rising anger in the voice, but Frank was
not keen enough to detect it.

"I'm coming. Don't fret yourself. But
here——catch!" cried the boy unconcernedly,
tossing down the fine specimen of the American Erne as if it had been a bundle of
old rags.

"Oh, butter-fingers!" followed his first remark as a matter of course.

The astonished baronet—for it was Sir

Hector himself—had let the bird slip to the ground, though he made a vain attempt to save it—

"You insolent young jackanapes, I never in all my life met your equal in effrontery. Come down, I say, this instant."

Sir Hector's tone and manner did not augur well for Frank's happiness at Grims-wych Park.

"I will not tolerate you in my house, not for another second, sir."

"I'm sorry, I'm sure. I did not know I was doing wrong."

Sir Hector waved him grandly on one side, and said—

"Ring the bell, if you please."

The butler, when he appeared, looked curiously at Frank, as if to gather from his appearance how he had fared while on his trial in this the first interview.

There was no misunderstanding the boy's *gauche* attitude, his red cheeks, and the way he hung his head.

"Mr Wriottesley's portmanteau, is it un-packed?"

" It is, Sir Hector."

" Then repack it. This young gentleman will return to the station as soon as a carriage can come round. Order one. That will do."

Then turning to Frank he said severely—

" I am not going to have my house turned upside down by every idle, mischievous, young vagabond that chooses to presume on my good nature and his own bad breeding."

" I am not an idle young vagabond," said Frank, looking Sir Hector straight in the face. " If I have done any wrong I'll bear the brunt, but you shan't call me names."

" Hoity-toity! a nice way you must have been brought up. Is this the way you were taught to address your elders? Your father and mother cannot have done their duty by you."

" My father and mother are dead," cried Frank, the tears starting into his eyes. " You know that; and you'd better leave them alone —you've no right to talk of them like that, and—and—I won't let you."

A very brave and gallant little fellow

Frank looked as he stood there with flashing eyes and fists clenched.

Sir Hector was several inches above six feet in height, and the boy before him—still only a child—hardly reached to his waist. But he bowed his head accepting the rebuke, and said at once—

" I beg your pardon—I forgot."

Already in the short scene that had been enacted he was beginning to relax. Other boys that had come had been so desperately afraid of him. They cowered or cringed, and he hated the one form of attention as much as the other. Here now was only a mite of a boy standing up to him, contradicting him, teaching him good manners.

" But what now ? " asked Sir Hector quickly —seeing Frank pick up the bird and make towards the ladder.

" I was going to put the Erne back in its place."

" You know its name then ? How's that ? Ah ! I see it's marked on the pedestal."

" I've shot one before now with my own gun," said Frank superbly, scorning his uncle's

inuendo, "in the Canadian forest, with——
with my father."

" You can shoot then ? "

" I used to go out with—him."

Frank hated these references to the happy
past.

" And you can ride ? "

" There was no other way of getting about
till the snow came. I had a pony of my own,
and rode it almost before I could walk."

" A pony of your own ? And you can shoot,
and have made a bag of your own in the
Canadian forests. Do you know anything
of the fauna ? "

" Fauna ? "

" Beasts and birds ? Have you learnt no
Latin. Do you recognise any more of those
birds there in that case ? "

" I see the golden oriole, and the blue-bird,
and the scarlet runner, and "——

" The Whitechapel is at the door, Sir Hector," said the butler with an unmistakable grin.

" Send it back to the stable. Mr Wriottesley is going to stay, I hope, for a long
time," added Sir Hector graciously.

The battle was over, and victory remained with Frank.

From that time forth young Wriottesley took undisputed rank as Sir Hector's heir. There was no question about him, as there had been about other candidates. He had won his position with colours flying, bold front, and uncalculating courage. Sir Hector took to him in a way he had done with no one before. Charmed from the first by the lad's gallant spirit, his liking grew into a strong attachment as Frank developed* in pluck and independence of character. It pleased him to hear how forward the boy rode, and what an excellent shot he was. The future owner of Grimswych must be fit to fill the place of an English gentleman, and must excel in field-sports as became his station; and Frank, after the first trial of strength, gladly gave in to Sir Hector's whims, and sought by all the means in his power to please him. The ready submission and cheerful attachment of the one soon produced esteem and warm affection in the other.

Frank was equally popular with all the
retainers at Grimswych. Mr Butterfield the
butler alone remained on the defensive. He
looked upon Frank as an interloper, and
would have been glad to have ousted him
from favour. But he could not accomplish
this; and as time passed Frank went to
Eton, thence for a year to College. Just
before he was twenty Sir Hector bought him
a commission in a good regiment, determined
not to baulk the young man, as he had himself been disappointed in the choice of a
profession. Moreover, the life was that of a
gentleman, and would serve to pass the years
until it was time for Frank to marry and
settle at Grimswych Park.

So it came to pass that Frank Wriottesley
found himself at five-and-twenty in the Halberdiers at Gibraltar.

CHAPTER VIII.

MAD TO TRAVEL.

SINCE the events at San Roque already de-
tailed, Frank's eager energies found a fresh
outlet. His ambition now was to turn
Spaniard, and make himself master of the
language; to explore every corner near Gibraltar, first by the beaten track, then by
remote road or rugged mountain-path, finding
sport where he could, but disposed even
without that attraction to wander like some
new Quixote from village to village and from
town to town, till he came to know thoroughly
the ways and usages of Spanish life.

There are many who, without the predis-
posing causes that affected Frank Wriottesley,
are seized with this kind of fever. A certain
romance hangs about the very name of Spain;

it is familiar to us in well-known books, in
the pages of Le Sage, of Cervantes, and
Washington Irving.   Most of us have read
Prescott, have followed Ford in his endless
rambles; we are well acquainted with Byron's
" Childe Harold," and through him with Inez
and the ladies of Cadiz.   From Spain came
the nuts we crunched in early youth, and the
liquorice that blackened our devoted lips, just
as other vices, more culpable, leave their
marks on the votary's life.   To the young
soldier, again, Spain is pre-eminently hallowed
ground.   It was the battlefield of our forefathers, of the men whose names form part of
such glorious memories as Talavera, Salamanca,
Vittoria, Ciudad Rodrigo, Badajoz, and the
Pyrenees.   In more than one English home
are treasured the journals of those Peninsular
heroes.   The ink faded, the paper all yellow
and tattered, like the flags under which our
veterans fought; the original records these of
the doings which Napier has chronicled in
language that will live for ever.   Thus the
romance of history lends an additional charm
to a land overflowing already with interest

and attraction. To be at Gibraltar, so near to Spain, scarce a stone's-throw from Spanish sentries and Spanish rule, on ground that some might say is Spanish still, and ours but in trust, is to find one's self within a magic circle, under the influence of spells difficult to resist. Close at hand, like a volume asking but to be opened, lies an exciting field— not necessarily of adventure, but filled with new and varied impressions—and five min- utes will bear the traveller to the land of promise.

Frank Wriottesley threw himself with delight into the life that opened for him at this new station. The passion for adventure was with him inbred, and the seed sown in early youth was already a plant of vigorous growth when he came to man's estate. But the occasion for following the bent of his inclinations did not come to him at once. In England there had been many calls upon his time: Grims- wych Park and due service to his uncle; the shooting there and the hunting—all these hindered him from seeking to travel far afield. For it was not to follow by the ordinary routes, in the smooth footsteps of summer tourists, but to make more lengthy journeyings through less known lands, that Frank Wriottesley pined. Chance alone was wanted to make of him an African explorer or a shining light in the Alpine Club ; one who in the East might have run Burton hard for his laurels, or have braved dangers as unconcernedly as the most venturous travellers in the Far West. And for the first time something of this kind seemed within his reach. From the very windows of his barrack-room he could see the margins of two continents, noble hunting-grounds both, asking him but to choose between them. Across the Straits of Hercules lay Barbary, a sealed page still to English wanderers, tempting him to be the first to tread its soil. Nearer at hand were the Spanish sierras, coming down to the water's edge and displaying their purple beauties with a prodigal hand, showing their jagged tops and the clean-riven fissures between, leading to happy valleys cradled in plenty.

The meeting with Lola was the turning-point. He was now, so to speak, mad to travel in Spain.

Of course Frank threw himself into this new idea with all the impulsive ardour that was natural to him. And first, to save himself from guides and interpreters, gaining through them only a second-hand knowledge of the country, he resolved to learn the Spanish language as fast as he could. He was no great linguist—had no natural aptitude for languages, that is to say—and he detested books. But then he was always so terribly in earnest with anything he took in hand. This difficulty he grasped also, with characteristic force and energy.

Down Horse Barrack Lane, the second door on the left hand of the furthest *patio* (court), lived a certain Geromino Ciruelas, who styled himself on the board that graced the entrance to his dwelling, *Professor de Idiomas*, Language Master to the garrison of Gibraltar. A tall, oily wretch, with fat hands, and manners as greasy as his complexion, was Geromino Ciruelas. But him from henceforth Frank made his inseparable

companion.   Ciruelas complained of other
engagements ; Frank bought them all up,
and with them all the teacher's time, till
the latter became his property, a sort of
private chattel, like his watch or favourite
alarum, to be set going when and how he
pleased.

Frank hated books, as I have said, because
he disliked sedentary pursuits, and he now
ingeniously contrived to make Ciruelas an
admirable substitute for grammar, phrase-
book, and dictionary.   The two took long
walks together, scaling the steep fortress
roads, or lounging beneath the shady avenues
of the Alameda ; and Frank kept his master
to his work all the time.   Ciruelas had to tell
him first the Spanish names for everything
they saw, then the simpler forms of talk ;
and by and by as Frank's ears grew more
and more accustomed to the sound, to repeat
whole conversations which they overheard
sometimes in the market-place, sometimes
on the Old Mole, sometimes among the
crowds on the Alameda on band nights, or
in the streets.   Frank took Ciruelas with

him on guard, keeping him busy all day till the dogs—of whom several infest every guard-room ' on the Rock—barked at the gibberish which they heard.

There were many drawbacks to this un-intermittent companionship, but Frank was not to be set aside by trifles. Ciruelas was a presuming, underbred cad, who thought that Frank's eagerness for his society grew out of affectionate personal regard, and not at all from Frank's desire to learn Spanish quickly. So he treated our hero with an easy familiarity for which at other times he would have been incontinently kicked down stairs. Thus he would lounge into Frank's quarters with the air of a comrade, and as this was the hot season, would rapidly divest himself of half his attire in order to be quite at ease. First went the black shoe-string that did duty for a tie, the paper collar followed, and probably the soiled brown holland coat. Frank would find him some-times thus, in his room about the time of early dawn, after a week of unpunctuality, stretched at full length upon the sofa, and

L

languidly sweeping his fat fingers across the strings of a guitar.

"You are early this morning," Frank would perhaps remark in a tone of sarcasm.

"Early?." (he called it "airly"), "*Sí, Señor, tempranito,* a little early I am. God helps those that *madrugar,* that do the daylight trick. But you are not yet arisen? no matter" (with that air of good-natured superiority which early risers assume)—"It is no matter, I can wait."

Probably Ciruelas had been keeping it up all night, and had come straight from his revels—on *azucarillas* (sugar-rolls) and water —to give Frank his lesson. Often at first he sought also to do his toilette ablutions at Frank's expense, water being in those days scarce and somewhat of a luxury on the Rock.* A new notion—this washing—for which he deserved congratulation; but when he brought in a tumbler to be filled with water, and announced his intention of using

* In 1869, pure water was found in great quantities not many feet below the surface upon the north front. This is now conveyed by a system of pipes into the town, and furnishes an abundant supply.

it as a basin, Frank was constrained to use strong language, after which Ciruelas was insulted, and washed no more.

But not the less, for all his dirty ways and greasy familiarity, did Frank consort with Ciruelas. They were called the Corsican brothers, and were never seen apart. Time passed thus till Frank had obtained a certain command of Spanish small-talk, and now he was ambitious to test his knowledge. To do this and apply the necessary corrections, he insisted upon dragging Ciruelas with him into Spain. Not too willingly did the Spanish teacher consent to seat himself in the saddle. His mount was a big-boned yellow steed, named *Taraxicum*, as rough as a railway truck on a worn-out siding. Astride of this Ciruelas went to his fate. At first he found the motion not unpleasant; Taraxicum walked well, with high showy action, arching his proud crest and sweeping his long tail in magnificent curves, till Ciruelas felt himself a new Cid Campeador as he ran the gauntlet of the bright glances, darted through the half-closed green jalousies of

the principal street. But once through the
Spanish lines and out upon the beach, a
change came o'er the scene. Frank, when
the "going" was good and his horse fresh,
was always anxious to push on at a rapid
pace. Alas! what a falling off was there!
Ciruelas at first lay helpless like a big barrel
just cast loose upon the deck of a storm-
tossed ship, rolling next instant from side
to side, dashing up now against pummel then
against crupper, again caught up, so to speak,
in among the rigging, mixed up with mane
and reins and stirrups, clinging where he
could—till all at once his hold gave way
and he slipped off his horse, right into the
wave-foam that fringed the shore.

When the wretched preceptor had been
rescued by Frank and some passing *arrieros*
from a watery grave, he resolutely set his
face homewards, and refused to ride again.
Next day he and Frank had words; and
this, their first difference, grew through the
teacher's greed and rapacity into an open
rupture. One method by which Ciruelas
eked out his gains, was by selling books to

his pupils. These he made them buy not in cheap volumes but in *editions de luxe,* novels chiefly by the prolific Fernandez y Gonzalez, published in numbers and furnished each with a sensational copperplate ; so that though the *entrega*—the weekly part—cost but a few pence, the sum total rose soon to a goodly sum. Frank of all books hated most these yellow-backed pamphlets that littered all his rooms ; and when Ciruelas added to his con- tumacy in refusing to ride by presenting a long bill for his trashy novels, Frank's anger rose, and the Spanish master was forthwith bundled out of the place, neck and crop, his yellow *entregas* following him like the long train of a comet, in their fiery flight.

But in truth Frank felt himself strong enough by this time to be independent of his teacher's aid. Already he contemplated travel. Alone, for he wished to come and go as he pleased, halt here, push on there, or return on his steps, just as the spirit moved him. Moreover, when cut off from English-speaking companions, he would become daily more and more accustomed to the idiom of

the people by whom he was surrounded daily.
He made his plans rather secretly therefore,
obtained leave only at the last moment, and
before they knew at mess that he had started,
he had crossed the sands below the Queen
of Spain's Chair, and was half way to the
Venta de Rosario on the Guadiaro river,
where he meant to halt the night.

His point was Granada *via* Ronda; an
ascent of the Veleta or Muley Hacen in the
Sierra Nevada came within the programme,
and he thought of returning through Cordova
and Seville. A strong, compact Spanish horse,
with an ugly head but good clean legs,
carried him and his saddlebags, and when
he got beyond the beaten track, sniffing for
the first time the air of freedom, and of
change, he felt himself transported to another
world. Indeed, it is only to those who have
travelled through Southern Spain on horseback that there is meaning in the Spanish
word *caballero*—" gentleman "—the rider and
owner of a horse. He ought indeed to be
an open-hearted, high-couraged gentleman.
He is brought daily into the presence of

Nature's loveliest works, seen through the pure air of the lofty sierras or the softer atmosphere of the low-lying sunny plains. His road takes him through wide pastures dotted with herds, or along narrow lanes flecked by dancing shadows, under a natural arcade of wild vines, festooned with twining creepers, brightened by broad passion-flowers, honeysuckles, convolvuluses, and blush roses. Now he stumbles on the sharp, worn flints of some old paved road, or walking delicately among huge boulders, threads some half-dried watercourse breasting a waving sea of ole-anders. Again winning the toilsome ascent of one of the lesser mountain ranges, he looks down from his towering station among the vultures and the goats upon the fair scene unrolled below—a boundless expanse of hills spread out like a carpet at his feet. He is constantly in vigorous exercise; he spends his days in the saddle and in the open air; he sleeps the sleep of the innocent and the child; his digestion needs no dinner-pills, his appetite no pampering. No form of active enjoyment can be compared to such travelling, and Frank Wriottesley was at length in his glory.

Of this, the first of many similar journeys, let me pause to say a word. It was new to Frank, and may be also to many readers. For the true lover of Nature it was crowded with new sensations. First the road along the valley to Gaucin following the tortuous windings of the half-dried river's bed; then the great hill to the town, a wretched remnant of attempted Macadamisation, or old paved roadway, wherein at every step sharp-pointed boulders raise their heads to aggravate still further the labour to those who climb. Yet was not the reward, once gained, well worthy of the toil? All the leagues back to the Straits visible every inch, the whole space stretching out like a wide and variegated carpet, through which runs one silver thread, the river margined by vivid spots of yellow light, the ripening harvest, or the purple shadows of the dark-green trees. The atmosphere is clear, the sky calm, the distant sea like glass, beyond them again Apes' Hill and the African mountains—so far and yet so near. All at once, as we gaze, across the summit of the peak-shaped Rock, has gathered a small white cloud. The wind has gone round suddenly to the east, and the Levanter has begun. Just as rapidly the landscape changes; dull purples and dark iron greys succeed the azure in the sky; the clouds are ragged at the edges, a lurid light seems to illumine the far-off horizon; a long narrow streak of misty choking vapour rises gradually from the sea, and swallows up the African hills.

Again, the next day's ride; by the winding mountain path at a high level, not far above you the mountain-tops, below the valley a thousand feet down, teeming with richness, crowded with vineyards, thick with fruit-trees; while away beyond rolls a wide expanse of distance, range behind range dotted with white towns, each securely placed upon its own conical hill. A wild picturesque ride. Climbing, descending, up hills, down valleys, by misty obscure paths, the sloping sides of the mountains hidden sometimes by a curtain of swift-moving cloud. Yet not a lonely road : other travellers there are, traders with

horses carrying their goods; *arrieros* with
long strings of donkeys employed by others,
but at times loaded up with ventures of
their own; now and again a pig boy driving
his herd, or a man with a pair of mules,
his private property, bent on business of his
own—these, too, seen in positions the most
diverse, now down, down deep in the valley
bottom, next goat-like nearer the summit
coming like black specks across the white
light of the sky.

Or Ronda itself, Ronda the unrivalled,
in which are endless pictures from endless
points of view, varying with the ever-chang-
ing effects. Every group in the street
would be a study for John Phillip. At
every corner Murillo might have found
beggar-boys for subjects after his own heart,
and at intervals a glimpse of a female face
of the true Spanish type, of the same bright
beauty as in the days when the great painter
took his Madonnas from models of real flesh
and blood. All here is beautiful. Whether
from the lowest level, where the river flows at
last quiet and tranquil after its noisy career,

you look up at the bridge spanning the chasm with its daring arch; whether the eye wanders more at ease over the luxuriance of the foreground foliage, which almost hides the mill at the foot of the gorge; whether it is the dashing spray of the river tumbling over the precipice, or the gleam of intense cobalt through the openings of the arch, or the view from the old Moorish king's palace, with its detail of houses in the upper town; or whether at the main approach, before passing under the ancient gateway with its coat of arms, you come across the gossips at the well.

And there was more beyond. From Ronda riding towards La Pizarra, where there is a station upon the Cordova–Malaga line of rail, you traverse the pass and valley of El Burgo, renowned as one of the most magnificent prospects in Spain. As if to prepare the traveller for the wonders in store, and mark the stronger the contrast, the road to El Burgo is meagre and uninteresting, a series of mountain valleys, where all is poor and bare. The cold grey rocks stare through the scanty clothing of their verdure, that

clings hopelessly to their sides; patches of
blighted corn gave prospect of an empty
harvest. There are hardly any human beings
about in this deserted, solitary place. Passing
a watering-trough, one half-starved denizen
of the wilds is transferring the water from
the spring to the trough by means of a frying-pan, an ill-starred savage, whose garments
are a mass of pendulous rags, and who runs
at the sight of his fellow-man. A few yards
more, a short ascent, a short fall; again up,
and then there bursts upon the eye a view
of grandeur and beauty—a wide deep valley
like an enormous crater, not of volcanic origin,
or at least by this time the wastes of scoriæ
and wild igneous rocks have given place to
the most luxurious vegetation. The. slopes
teem with richness; on one side vineyards
climbing close to the mountain-tops, on the
other, where the gradient is more gradual,
corn and barley were thriving, while upon
every flat surface long lines of olive grove
laid upon the lesser hills looked like table-
cloths of curious stuff studded with little
round balls.

Pages might be filled with the description of that which Frank encountered; but this is not a guide-book to Andalucia, and I have lingered only because this first journey had no little effect in developing certain traits of our hero's character. Frank through it all, it must be confessed, was an object of wonder and surprise to all who met him in Spain. The natives by the wayside gaped and gazed at him with open-mouthed astonishment, for Frank as often as not preferred to walk, and drove his horse in front of him, like an Irishman taking his pig to the Fair. At the posadas where he halted, this horse of his was his first care; no other hand but his made fast the headstall to its peg; he alone removed the saddle, gave out the feeds, and led the horse to water. Frank never thought of himself till he had washed out feet and used curry-comb and brush, generally before an amazed audience, who had never seen a horse thus groomed in all their lives. After that, he darted off to the kitchen, where the cook would be busy shredding garlic into a pipkin, and take this job also into his own hands. With his vigorous interference and masterful manners he inspired respect, but it was not a little the awe that simple, ignorant people feel for those who are slightly crazed. Nothing short of madness, they thought, could tempt a man, an Englishman, and therefore a Crœsus, or one who had made a voyage to the Indies, to work for himself. Laziness with them meant good-breeding, and their gentlemen often went nearer starvation than was pleasant sooner than soil their hands. But here was a *caballero* who toiled like a peasant. Assuredly he must be mad. Other symptoms were diagnosed as he got further along the road. At Coin they thought him mad because he did not shudder at the danger of the Ojen Pass, a narrow gorge crowded with *mala gente*, who would have him " mouth downwards " faster than they fry eggs. Mad at Monda, on the journey home, because he stripped to bathe in the roaring *douche* beneath the halted mill-wheel ; mad at Antequera, because he forced the barber into his own chair and taught him how to shave ; the same at Arola, because he kissed the hostess and paid a uinous bill, thereby proving the truth of he Spanish proverb that a pretty landlady is bad for the pocket. At Ronda he was thought mad because he showed the farrier how to shoe a horse; at Loja, because he preferred the saddle, and rode on although he railway ran side by side with the road. At Granada appeared the worst paroxysms of lunacy. He must needs climb the snow mountains behind the town. Was it not enough for him to gaze up at them from below, as the good Granadinos had done since birth, from generation to generation?

But there was a method in this madness. When Frank got back to Gibraltar, after a month's absence, he knew more of Spain, its people, and its language, than many tourists after years of travel.

CHAPTER IX.

A SPANISH VAGABOND.

As the summer drew on towards its close, so Josefa's furlough at San Roque came to an end. But by this time the health of her son Pepe was nearly restored, though he was still a little weak from his recent hurts. His mother was therefore eager to get him some employment, something that might preserve him from a relapse into his late dangerous trade, and if possible to keep him for the future by her side. Whether she could hold the vagrant fast was not so certain; for Pepe was a vagabond by profession, partly from circumstances, partly from decided inclination for the trade. For years past he had wandered about in Spain, a good-for-nothing, idle scamp, sometimes up in the world, generally down.

If there were streaks of luck in his life, they were rare—rare as the slices of lean in the fat bacon he loved to eat with his beans—when he could get it. And for the slackness of his bringing-up, Josefa, though just now very affectionate, was mostly to blame. In the debtor and creditor account between mother and son, the latter owed the former little on the score of maternal attachment.

Pepe drew breath and spent his earliest days in a spacious edifice by the shores of Gibraltar Bay — a residence built of mud and old wine-cases, with one of Huntley and Palmer's biscuit-boxes for a chimney. There are hundreds of such dwelling-places squatted around the big Rock, standing singly or in clusters. That belonging to Pepe's mamma —father he never knew—hung close to the skirts of Puente Mayorga, a hamlet named after the bridge hard by, which connected anywhere with nowhere, and spanned a sluggish stream, passable at all points without its aid. The hut, just above high-water mark, lay buried in heavy sand, and surrounded by a small wilderness of a garden, wherein, amidst

filth and fish-bones, the carcases of dead dogs
or horses slain in the bull-ring at Algeciras
or San Roque, occasionally festered and bore
unsavoury fruit.   Behind, the sharp spikes
of the ragged aloe-hedge blossomed on wash-
ing-days with clothes of bright colour.   One or
two *faluchas*—mediæval boats, with spars
like the antennæ of a curious spider—were
drawn up on the beach; for Puente Mayorga
lived by the products of the sea, legal or contraband.   Pepe's father had been one of these
free-traders, hauling his net in by day, and
running cargoes by night, till a carabinero's
bullet put an end to his life, and made him
pay all back dues in person.   Since then the
bread-winning had fallen upon the surviving
parent, the Tia Josefiya, who trudged daily
into the garrison with prickly pears or freshly-
caught sardines.   Pepe, thus left much to
himself, played about stark naked in company
with dozens of other brats as brown-skinned
and bullet-headed as himself; burrowing knee-
deep in the sand, rushing in and out of the
stream, or offering themselves up as willing
sacrifices to the English officers from the Rock,

seeking martyrdom under the hoofs of these galloping Juggernauts, who tore along the beach at sundown—a practice in which they were encouraged by their parents, since the indemnity, extorted in case of accident, would have kept Puente Mayorga in affluence for years.

Neglected and uncared for, Pepe grew up like a little savage. He was surrounded by scenes of beauty, but they made no more impression upon him, as he lay curled up like a ball upon the beach, than if he had been a zoophyte, or a withered leaf, or an unfledged bird peeping over its nest among the tree-tops, and gazing down with calm unconsciousness upon the plays of light and shadow, rich colouring and marvellous beauty of form, in the valleys and hillsides below. It was as nothing to him—insignificant brown mite that he was—that the sun set in splendour night after night behind the purple mountains. These crimson and golden glories might light up his childish eyes with gladness at their opalescent hues, but they did not speak to him, as they might to other children, of the high and heavenly mysteries of those radiant halls, where dwelt, far withdrawn, the spirits of the blest. Nor was the evening lustre of the smooth and silent Bay a source of pleasure to him, unless it was calm enough for the porpoises to come close in shore, and break the surface of the water into dancing ripples of rose-tinted mother-of-pearl. Still less did he care for the tender hopefulness of the early dawn; all that he knew was that he had been roused too soon from his infantile slumbers, and his bleared and gummy eyes, ophthalmia-afflicted already from the fine particles of sand with which every breeze was laden, refused to greet the rising sun with either gratitude or satisfaction.

Perhaps the only scene that distinctly affected him was the ceremony of drawing in the nets. He would sit for hours watching the men in perpetual procession walk away with the never-ending rope, till at last the heavily-laden meshes approached the sloppy shore, and then dance with yells of fiendish delight around the glittering, palpitating silver heap, that spoke to him of broiled fish for supper, possibly of a handful of clammy

sweet-stuff next day, when his mother came
back from the Rock after a successful sale.
Perhaps, too, after nightfall, if he was not
already asleep, he looked with something like
awe at the great black Rock, that loomed in
the distant moonlight with mysterious grandeur, for this was the great centre of life for
Puente Mayorga, making its influence felt
even by such as Pepe Picarillo. It had gates
that refused admittance to the misconducted,
and buyers for his mother's fruit, mountains
also of untaxed tobacco and salt, which she
brought away concealed in her stockings, so
that her legs seemed to suffer from elephanti-
asis.   According as trade was good or bad
upon the Rock, his mother smiled or swore ;
and it was held up to him as his highest hope
of future reward that he might some day be
taken there to see the soldiers in petticoats,
the shop-fronts, and the great cannons on its
walls.

But Pepe grew on, heedless for the most
part of all beyond the hours for feeding, naked
and shirtless, until the time arrived when he
was too big for such slender apparel, and he

was promoted to his first suit of clothing—a
cast-off red jacket from the garrison hard by,
which fitted him loosely from throat to ankle,
and was generally so irksome that he would
have cursed the memory of our first parents
had he ever learnt such elementary facts as
the fall of Adam and Eve from fig-leaves and
primitive innocence. Thus apparelled, Pepe
was bound apprentice to his first trade—that
of begging for cigar-ends and half-farthings
from the passers. But as fortune was dawning upon him to the tune of half a *peseta*,
or fourpence, laboriously earned, his mother
swooped down upon his store, transferring
every copper to her private purse, and
giving him in exchange a sound thrashing for
his reluctance in surrendering the coin. Next
day Pepe left his home, and started business
on his own account. At first, fearful of re-
capture, he fled to the recesses of the Cork
Wood, where he fought for his food for a
time with the acorn-eating pigs. From this a
passing turkey-seller took him to assist in
driving his flock into Gibraltar. Pepe made
two journeys, carefully avoiding Puente Ma-

yorga, but on the third met his mother face
to face at the inner gate of the fortress. She
cut him dead; and from henceforth Pepe felt
emancipated. He might have lived and died
a turkey-seller, had not the Inspector of Mar-
kets caught him cramming sand down the
throats of his live stock to increase their
weight. For this act, which his master repu-
diated, the lad was summarily ejected from
the garrison. That night he shipped on board
a *falucha* trading in mysterious cargoes to
the Spanish coast; a black, lateen-rigged
craft, which crept out towards sundown with
long sweeps, close in under the Rock, and
then dashed on as fast as wind and tide could
carry them, to make good a landing somewhere between Torre Nueva and Estepona.
After a dozen prosperous voyages, Pepe bid
fair to be as successful a smuggler as his
father; but fate again interposed. A fast-
sailing *escampavia* (revenue boat) ran in and
boarded the *falucha* before they could sink the
tell-tale bales.

Six months in a dungeon of the common
jail at Algeciras sickened Pepe of smuggling.

Discharged penniless and in rags, he was for weeks on the verge of starvation. At one time he thought of returning to his mother, like a bad farthing; but still he hung about the beach at Algeciras, picking up a job among the boats, or helping to drive the donkies the English visitors rode to the great waterfall behind the town. Then, when Fairtime came, he attached himself to Doña Eustaquia, a maker of *bunuelos*, or sweet cakes, thinking that though not the rose, he might live near it, and if he could not eat cakes all day long, he might at least smell them. With his new mistress he journeyed from town to town till they reached Ronda in the heart of the Sierra. Here one night, as he lay coiled up under the canvas booth, he heard them driving in the bulls for the next day's fight. They were close at hand. He could plainly hear the bells of the *cabestros*, or tame oxen, luring the bulls on, the shouts of the herdsmen, the occasional bellow of the fierce beasts that were being driven in to their death. Pepe, , true Spaniard, went forward to watch; and as he stood there it

struck him that, failing money to buy himself
a ticket next day, he might stow himself
away inside and wait, concealed till the hour
of the performance. As the process of shutting up the bulls (the *encierro*) is an anxious
operation, needing all the care of those employed, no one noticed Pepe sneaking in. He
hid himself beneath a bench and slept till
morning, when his slumbers were rudely dis-
turbed by a stout twig of green olive in the
hands of the *impresario*, who had discovered
the stowaway.

" Little blackguard ! How did you get in
here ? "

" At the *encierro*."

" Then march. Quick ! *Estas ?* "

" No, señor, no. I am a poor orphan, and
I am *aficionado*, devoted to bull-fights."

The idea was a good one. This ragged
little wretch a patron and supporter of the
sport !

" Are you ready to work ? "

" *Ya lo creo*." ("I believe you.")

" And not afraid ? "

" Not of the devil himself."

" Well, go down to the stables and help."

So Pepe was forthwith engaged to assist the purveyor of horseflesh to the ring. His new duties might have shocked a more fastidious mind. Armed with a stout stick, he belaboured the tottering charger that refused to face the horns; with nimble hands he hustled back the entrails torn out in each mad onslaught, or kicked a prostrate horse on to his legs again, when seemingly at the last gasp. Then, when each bull was slain, he brought the baskets of dry earth to soak up the blood that gathered in dark pools about the arena. Outside he worked with needles and thread and wads of cotton to patch up the wounds of horses not quite killed, yet doomed to endure the horrors of a second death. He enjoyed his life thoroughly, and made great progress. Now and again he held on by the *picador's* stirrups; more than once he touched the bull's hindquarters or his tail. By and by his zeal and energy met with their reward. One of the *toreros* (bull-fighters), pleased with his prowess, engaged him as personal attendant, and

taught him all he himself knew of the trade.
By degrees Pepe came to take a more pro-
minent part in the performances, at first with
the *novillos*, or young bulls, then with the
" bulls of death." It was a pleasant life;
money came in fast; he made enough through
the summer season to keep him in idleness
all the winter months. He was lucky; others
came to grief, but Pepe saw the end of many
a hard-fought day without a scratch. At
length at San Roque his turn came, and he
nearly met his death. Now, he had no great
desire to resume the *rôle* of a *picador*, and
gladly seconded his mother's efforts to get
him work.

First, Josefa went to her own master. Don
Mariano met her with abuse.

" What! I support the rogue! Am I so
rich that I can take in every woman's son
because she asks me? *Vaya!*"

" He has been ill."

" A bad son is better ill than well."

" Do not double the burthen of a loaded
mule. Say you will help an unfortunate
mother in her distress."

"The times are hard; let every one scratch himself with his own nails. With eating and scratching the only thing is to begin."

"But, señor, give him work; take him into your service."

"Give him a chance of robbing me, you mean."

"My son is no *pillo* (thief)."

"I wouldn't take your word for it. A good-for-nothing idler, who spends his time propped against walls to keep them from falling."

"I did not think you were so stingy. It's well you're not the sun, or you would be too stingy to warm us."

"Stingy! because I will not throw away my substance upon this *pan perdido*, this lost bread, upon whom good food is wasted!"

"What fly has stung you, master? Have I not served you faithfully? Cannot you trust my recommendation?"

"A mother's swans are the worst of geese. But tell me, then, what is he good for? Can he keep accounts, and write and cipher, and speak English?"

"He never had much schooling, but he can ride and groom a horse."

"Is my stable, then, so full of horses that I want a dozen *mozos*? Have I perchance a squadron of cavalry to my own cheek? Am I the Governor of this fortress, or the second chief, or one of those spendthrift officers, that I must waste my dollars on other mouths, on barley for beasts, when I have barely bread for me and my own? Groom a horse! *Caramba*, a pretty recommendation to me, who never owned a nag since I sold the grey *tordo* to feed the English fox dogs."

"The Señorita Dolorcita will be coming back from Ximena soon, and she has learnt to ride. You said she was to learn and if she has a horse"——

"*Oye*, listen, woman. Dost think me a fool? Is my face as mad as a monkey's? My pearl may ride, if she likes, a dozen steeds, the best that money can buy her, but she rides with her equals, as she will mate. I want no brown-faced *mozo* to make sheep's-eyes at her as he lifts her into the saddle, to hang about her till perchance she forgets herself and her station.. The game is too· high. Those who cannot walk had best not try to fly."

"The saints defend me, Señor *mio!*" cried Josefa, crossing herself. "You're more change-able than a weathercock or a windmill. Your tongue stings like a bee's tail."

"*Mira!* I know what I am about. Make yourself like sugar and the flies will come to eat you. I will be master in my own house. The lunatic is more powerful in his own than Solomon in anybody else's. No more. Seek another *amo* for your precious son; he comes not here. One of your family is somewhat too much for me as it is."

Josefa was crestfallen, but not yet despon-dent. She had another strong card to play which might turn the game to Don Mariano's disadvantage. Her intention was now to sell herself, so to speak, to the enemy.

Frank Wriottesley a day or two later was in the anteroom recounting his recent ad-ventures when a mess-waiter came up and whispered—

"A female, sir, below, at the door; she was wishing to speak with you."

"A female? to see me?" asked Frank, rather incautiously, aloud, thereby drawing down upon himself the attention of the whole mess.

"Don't mind us!" cried Sproule amidst general laughter. "What is she like, Glubb?"

"A native, sir; leastways she's not a European, sir; that is, she don't speak English."

This man had been long in India, and he had got a notion that Spaniards, as foreigners, should be classed with black Asiatics.

"They didn't teach you much geography, Glubb," said Honeybun.

"Never mind, Glubb. You're not the first person who has called Spain Oriental," remarked Frank.

"Wriottesley wants to turn the subject. I vote we go with him to interview the European."

So in a body they trooped downstairs like schoolboys, some sliding by the banisters, others whooping and shouting, and hustling Frank along five steps at a time.

"Here he is, ma'am!" shouted the leading one. "He's shy, but that'll wear off. Don't mind us; we've only come to see fair play."

It was Josefa, dressed in her Sunday best, but not attractive in appearance in spite of all her finery. Yet with native dignity she put the tormentors on one side and went up to Frank, touching him playfully with her fan while she wreathed her lips into a smile, saying, in Spanish—

"*Señor de mi alma !* my soul's lord! Of your amiability and condescension have compassion upon a miserable woman. If you would gain happiness in this life and salvation in that which is to come, if you would avoid sleepless nights in this world, and shorten, by my intercession, the hours of purgatory in the next, I pray you grant me one favour!"

Frank easily understood that Josefa wanted something, and as all she had said was so much High Dutch to the others, he replied, as far as he was able, in her own language. The others, finding the interview promised to be slow, soon sheered off.

"What can I do to help you, señora?" asked Frank.

"Sir, I have a son,—a youth of ingenuous and sympathetic disposition, skilled in every art, in demeanour gracious, in temper angelic. He is tall, and—I cry your pardon—though a mother speaks, handsome as the summer flowers."

"Señora," replied Frank, rising to the occasion, "that you are most fortunate, I need not say. But with such a mother, what should not the offspring be! May his future be as prosperous as his deserts seem to entitle him. It is of this excellent youth that you would now speak?"

"By your amiability, yes," cried Josefa, simpering and casting down her eyes. "This son is the star of my life, who has all that heaven can give him, save one boon alone"——

"And that is?"

"Your worship's protection."

Frank did not see his way at all clearly, and he was compelled to change his tone.

"Señora, I beg of you to speak more plainly. The sun is already on the slope, and your words are as obscure as the darkness that must soon overtake us. What can I do for your son ?"

"Take him—keep him. May he bring you a blessing!" said Josefa, with tears now in her eyes, as she made a present of this priceless gift to Frank.

"Pardon me, madam ; you will forgive my reserve"——

People are not in the habit of giving away their children, except at a tender age, in omnibuses or on door steps, and Frank hesitated.

"You will excuse me if I decline the gift. Of what earthly use would this interesting and amiable youth be to me ?"

"Make him groom your horses and ride them ! Ah, what a horseman is there !" said the mother picturing to herself Pepe's seat and graceful bearing in the saddle.

"He is a groom then ?" For the first time a light was breaking in on Frank.

"Of the best, señor ; he has not his equal in Spain."

"But I want no servant at present. I am

well suited, nor do I think just now of adding to my stable."

"Señor," put in Josefa, "if I mistake me
not, your worship was at San Roque at the
Fair?"

"Yes!"

"I saw you. When would my eyes forget
such manly beauty, such stout splendour of
form and feature?" Flattery is a ready
weapon with women of Josefa's nation and
class. "I saw you from the first, but then
my Pepe was hurt in the ring below, and
close by my side my little mistress swooned,
and I was like to go mad with fear of
losing both."

"Fainted, you say? The young lady who
fainted, was that the same that I myself
carried out of the ring?"

"My master's granddaughter, señor—the
Señorita Doña Maria de los Dolores Bellota
y Peñaflor."

Frank in the months that had passed had
far from forgotten Lola, but as time went
by his chance of again meeting her seemed
to grow more and more remote. But now,

thus unexpectedly, all at once upon the
trail.

" And you ? " Frank asked.

" I am Don Mariano's hands and feet,
ama de llaves, key-mistress and custodian
of Don Mariano's house, caretaker also of
his pearl, the choice child of his heart,
Dolorcita, the star of my life."

" Is the young lady well ? "

" Fairly so, but delicate as a dove, fragile as
a spray of jasmine. She dreams only of you."

As Josefa had not seen Lola since the
time of the bull-fight, she made this statement quite without foundation ; nor had she
the least compunction about sacrificing the
child's maidenly reserve to gain her own
selfish ends.

" And where does she now reside ? Here,
upon the Rock ? " asked Frank with as un-
concerned an air as he could assume.

" Señor, at Ximena ; my son Pepe could
point out the very spot where she is to be
found."

" I understand. The road is difficult and
needs a practised guide ? "

" Precisely, señor *mio ;* your worship is sharper than a bolster. A guide you must have. I offer Pepe. *Está usted?* Is it a bargain ? "

It was; and within a week Frank, accompanied by his new groom, was on his way to Ximena. Thither let us precede him, and look in on the place which for these few months past Lola had made her home.

Life at Agua Dulce was very tranquil, indeed, a trifle slow. Ximena, the nearest town, was a dull place, stagnant, ruinous, off the highroad, and unfrequented. There was little employment or amusement, either, for Lola, except to watch the flowers in the garden grow, or take a lesson from ¬her cousin Lucas in horsemanship. This riding on a side-saddle gave mortal offence to Doña Teresa, whose conservatism would have made it penal for any one to seek to improve upon the ways of their grandmothers. Still less could she tolerate the grey riding-habit, the "Amazona," as it is called in Spanish, which Lola had brought with her from Gibraltar. As for the pantaloons and the man's hat—for our little heroine carried her imitativeness of the English ladies to the last extreme—these new-fangled notions gave Doña Teresa a *jaqueca*, a headache, which lasted her for a week. The only consolation to be found in this new fancy of Lola's was, that it threw her in the way of Lucas, the eldest-born and heir to the cortijo, for whom the little heiress would have been an unmistakable "catch." Indeed, while Lola was still a child, Doña Teresa had sought to come to terms with old Bellota, endeavouring to bind him thus early to an engagement. But Don Mariano had protested that his granddaughter should choose for herself when the time came, and would make no promise. Nevertheless, he sent Lola year after year to the farm, and was for ever talking to her of her cousins, as if he wished her to take a fancy to one or other of them. Therefore it was that Lola—with the wilfulness of her sex and under the wayward fate that governs such matters—fell in love with Frank Wriottesley.

In the daytime the members of the family

did not meet much, except at meals, and these were soon despatched. It was not until towards sundown that they gathered together around the big entrance gates, over which hung their colossal coat of arms, "to take the fresh," as they called it, and talk. These evening meetings out of doors are the substitutes in Andalucia for the open air "at homes," or *tertulias*, which the grandees of Spain give upon the Prado at Madrid. The upper folk entertain thus any passing friend. Among the peasantry, the wife and daughter, mother and maidens, sit by the door to welcome home the bread-winner returning from his labour in the fields, while the little ones rush forward to get between their father's legs or scramble on to his patient donkey's back. These peaceful parties are in keeping with the tranquil hour, the fading light, the growing stillness, which nothing breaks but the voices of the sitters, the tinkle of a distant bell, or the monotonous chant of an *arriero* on the road, keeping time to the measured pace of his slowly-jogging mule. Then, in the midst of all their talk, the deep-toned church-bell proclaims the *animas*, the evening hour of prayer for the dead. The men uncover their heads, the women tell their beads aloud, and the children pause in their play to whisper that the angels are close at hand.

The ladies of Agua Dulce, Doña Teresa, Ramona, and Lola, seated thus on low chairs by the doorway, are hearing the day's news. Miguel has been up to the town, a mile or two distant, and has returned brimful of gossip.

" Listen, ma'am," he says to his mother. " There is good news from Alcalá. They say the barley crop has failed."

" Do you call it good news to hear that your neighbours are ruined ? " asked Lola.

" *Vaya !* " Doña Teresa observed ; " we must all live. Our barley here was abundant."

" One man eats sour fruit and another gets the toothache. Luck is not the same for all."

"August and harvest do not come every day, but once a year; sometimes in plenty, sometimes not at all," said Ramona.

" And, Dolorcita," went on Miguel, " there are *titeres* (acrobats) coming—Americans with an insect."

" A *bicho*! Does it sting ? "

" No, *hija:* it is an elephant, and it will fight with a bull."

" Ah ! " said Lola with a shudder.

" Not recovered yet! " cried Ramona. " Perchance you will again faint, and this time there may be no one by to give you succour."

At which Lola blushed, for it brought back to memory an incident and individual both of which she had tried hard to forget.

" *Mas* " (more), went on Miguel; " I saw to-day that *picador*, your dueña's son, who was injured at the last San Roque fight."

" Pepe ! He is alive then and well ? "

" What brings him hither ? " asked the mistress. " Are we to have a *funcion* here ? I had not heard of it."

" A bull-fight in this corner of the earth," cried Ramona. " Sooner would the skies rain silk handkerchiefs and silver combs."

" Of course not. Pepe has turned groom. He is servant to a señor who has come out from Gibraltar to buy horses."

" To buy horses ? " cried Lucas, who with his brother Alejandro at that moment came upon the scene. " Then we can suit him here. Have I not ten *potros* (steeds) for sale ; of race, pure blood, and of the finest Cordovan breed ? I can fit him with what he wants as oil does spinach."

" Is he a stranger ? " asked Doña Teresa.

" I did not see him ; but Pepe said he was a *rico*, a man with dollars ; but intelligent in horse-dealing."

" English, then, or *Gibraltareño ?* "

" He speaks Castilian."

" *Ea !* " burst in Alejandro ; " the Spanish they talk on the Rock would not pass at the Court of Madrid."

Alejandro had seen the world—of Spain, and was just now on leave of absence from his regiment.

Why was Lola's heart thumping against her side ? The visits of horse-dealers were not uncommon at the cortijo, but those who generally came belonged to the lower class, this one travelled with his servant and was an Englishman. What if ?——

" And did you forget to tell this Pepe to come out here with his master ? " asked

Lucas, with the contemptuous air he assumed always when speaking to his little brother. "You did? what more? Are you not proud of this wise son of yours, ma'am? Little idiot! not fit to take care of geese on a road," he added between his teeth.

"Why, what matter?" put in Ramona in Miguel's defence—the women fought for the little chap as they do for all who seem weak and oppressed. "Cannot you go yourself and tell him?"

"*I* go, and look anxious to sell, and•so depreciate my stock! Sister Ramona, you are wellnigh as dense as this small lump of foolishness."

"He is as good as you, small as he is," cried Lola. "Don't mind the bully, Miguelito. I cannot understand why he is always so unkind to you."

"Why?" said Lucas, crossing over to Lola and whispering in her ear. "Because you favour him, Dolorcita, and that makes me mad. Why is it you never smile on me?"

"You must mend your ways, Lucas, if you would kiss my hand," replied Lola with spirit. " I was not meant to be any man's obedient, humble slave—least of all, yours, my cousin. If you treat your brother thus, what might not I expect ? "

" To be the light of my eyes, the breath of my nostrils "——

" Pouf ! " interrupted Lola ; " keep such talk for the damsels up yonder in the town. Don't waste your words in flattering me."

" Is it that you love some one else, Lola ? " asked Lucas fiercely. " Tell me but his name, and by the life of the holy men I will squeeze him like a sponge."

" When the Moor has bolted a tremendous lance-thrust ; much cry and little wool, Lucas. The enemies you killed I'd eat, without one clove of garlic for sauce."

" Fighting, quarrelling always," said Doña Teresa. The prospect of Lucas and Lola coming together often seemed more than improbable.

" Señora," Lola cried, " he should have been a soldier, this Lucas. He was born to fight battles. Look how he conquers us women and Miguel "——

"Ah, truly!" observed Alejandro, who was fond of talking and had a long leeway to make up. "The life of John Soldier is a king's life. He sees the world, and knows how many make five. In the towns, *tertulias*, reunions, bull-fights, loves — and then the column marches, and he breaks fresh ground. To-day he is at Seville upon the Delicias, or up and down the Sierpes making eyes at all who pass; threading the busy Zacatin upon the Vivarrambla, or by the banks of flowery Darro, just under the snow-mountains that give the Granadinas grace and crimson cheeks; out among the gardens and plenty of Valencia, through the palm-forests of Elche, in bustling Barcelona, beneath the trees upon the Rambla, at the Court itself—at Madrid, where the Queen—whom God preserve! — keeps high festival."

"Perchance also at Melilla or at Ceuta, in a *presidio*, a prison-fortress, guarding convicts —what then? Is that so joyful?"

"Ay, there too. We hunt the wild boar, and sally forth to beard the Moorish warriors as did Los Reyes the Kings of Aragon and Castille."

" Have you slain many boars ? "

" Thousands ! " the truth being that Alejandro, when quartered upon the rocky peninsula of Ceuta, had never stirred forth beyond the gate of the little fortress-town. To mount guard, play dominoes, and make paper cigarettes, had fully occupied all his time.

" And you had a new *novia* (love) in every town ? " asked Miguel, wishing such luck was his.

" Yes. Loves—loves more stormy than the wintry seas. In Murcia, a duel to the death ; in Zaragossa, quarrels to make my hair turn grey—in Toledo, I jumped from a balcony higher than the belfry of our holy church "——

"Son, you might spare us these experiences," said Don Teresa primly. " Such tales would suit the barrack best, or the *corps de garde.*"

" It is a wonder you are here to speak of them," Lola said with a mischievous gleam in her eyes. "Such hair-breadth escapes, such harrowings of the heart."

" *Si, señora,* yes, madam, you may well

show wonder. In that last affair I was truly near my death. But," looking round for admiration, "I carry her memory, her picture engraven here," as he pointed to his watch-pocket, "and this token of her unalterable affection;" whereupon he produced a dirty rag of a pocket-handkerchief and kissed it devoutly. "It has never left me; day and night I wear it. It is months, years since we met, and still"——

"It looks as if it had better go to the wash," said Lola. "Can't you trust it to a laundress?"

"I have washed it with my tears," went on Alejandro.

"You must have had your eyes filled with dust and wept mud," said Lucas. "Who is this precious dame? Has she a portion enough to gain you your licence to marry?"

"She is penniless, but of angelic form and virgin beauty. Her father keeps a glove-shop in Cordova. I am ready to die for her, and for my country, like every true and loyal Spaniard."

"I believe you," said Lucas in a sneering

tone. He was jealous of his youn ger brother,
and owed him more than one bad turn,
"Fine patriots, you and the rest of your
cloth, that suck the best blood of this mis-
governed, impoverished land.   Where are
your glories gained ?   Against one another,
with your cursed insurrections and mutinies
playing into bad men's hands.   The enemy
you fight are your own comrades, or the poor
misguided people that you massacre to serve
the ends of the monster in power."

"We are for the cause of order always."

"Never, unless it suits you.   You are only
for gambling and idleness, until some schem-
ing revolutionist or pretender to power comes
and tampers with you, and then you scheme
too, and lead on your men—not to their
duty, but to fight for some blood-stained
butcher like Narvaez or O'Donnell.   If this
be your patriotism "——

"Heavens above!" cried Doña Teresa,
turning pale with affright, "can I believe
my ears ?   To use such language in these
days !   Do you value your throat ? or is
Agua Dulce so tame that you pine for the

Phillipines or the Canaries? These ages past have we been loyal all: in our family have been many high officials. My mother's brother was fiscal to the Judge of Segovia; your grandfather was customs collector in Cuba; your uncle, administrator of waste lands in La Mancha. We are honoured people, and I pray God my sons may never mix in low intrigues or lend themselves to plots against the Queen, the constitution, and "——

" The priests, you'd better add, madam," went on Lucas. " Your friends the priests, who keep you in the straight path to heaven, and who will gladly lend a hand to save Alejandro from perdition here and hereafter."

Lucas was country-bred and coarse, but he was keen-witted enough to see the ills from which Spain suffered. But, like every Spaniard not himself in power, he attributed all to the existing regime. His panacea was a change of government, forgetting that change had followed change a dozen times already, but in spite of all, the condition of the country remained the same.

But his violent outburst was unexpected, and rather chilled his audience.

The family talked little afterwards, and soon entering the house, partook of a frugal supper, then separated for the night.

CHAPTER X.

SPANISH COURTSHIP.

EARLY next morning they came to Lola and told her that Pepe, Josefa's son, was at the farm, and wished to see her. He had already arranged with Don Lucas to bring Frank out later in the day.

"Señorita, I lay myself at your feet," exclaimed Pepe with a low obeisance to Lola. "My mother bid me come to present her respectful wishes for your health and happiness."

"I am glad to hear you are strong and well, Pepe. And your mother? she has left San Roque?"

"She has returned to the dwelling of the good man that gives her bread."

"Are there no news yonder on the big Rock?"

"None; all is as dull as ditch-water."

"And you are travelling now from town to town in search of horses, my cousin tells me."

"The master that I serve is a *milor*, an English prince, whose gold flows from his purse fast as the water oozes from a rocky spring. He is in search of horseflesh—yes; but of yet more." Pepe looked round cautiously, as if he dreaded to be overheard. "He has come to find the true queen of his life, the rare flower whose fragrance shall preserve him from despair and death."

Pepe inherited his hyperbole from his mother.

Lola was taken aback, and shrunk from the man who spoke in such familiar terms.

"Am I indiscreet? Forgive me, Señorita; but he has come—under my guidance—for one purpose alone—to see you."

"I cannot see him—I do not know him. Who is he?"

"The hero of the ring—that English officer

who rescued your precious person when life threatened to become extinct. Shall I bring him this way?" went on Pepe, seeing Lola did not answer. "It will be easy to frame an excuse. Are there not at Agua Dulce horses unequalled this side of Jaen or Ante-quera? He shall come this very day to see them."

Lola instinctively, and with the fine feeling that was natural to her, disliked the idea of making any appointment to meet Frank Wriot-tesley. Whether she would have resisted a personal appeal was not so certain, but she was positive in her refusal to accept Pepe's connivance or help.

"If your master desires to see my cousin's stock, you need not ask my leave. Give your message straight to the *aperador* (the groom of the stables), or to Don Lucas himself."

"But it is you, and you only, that he longs to see."

"*Citas* (appointments) of such a kind are not made by my mother's daughter. *Hijo!* march—go elsewhere. I walk too high to

stoop to such baseness." And with that
Lola gave a magnificent sweep with her fan
towards the outer gate of the Cortijo, thus
letting Pepe plainly understand that he might
disappear as soon as he pleased.

Rather disconcerted, he retraced his steps
to the *posada*, where he found Frank waiting.

" Have you spoken to her ? "

" *Sì*, Señor, certainly."

" And she will see me ? "

" Of course. You are more than a bundle of
straw in her eyes. Of course she will see you."

" When and how ? "

Pepe had prepared his story.

" We are to go there again about noon to
see the horses. And, Señor, you might do
much worse. There is one among them fit
for a prince. The *amo* himself rides it, and
will hardly sell under a high figure—a horse
of race, a half-bred barb, that flies faster
than the swallow southward. Ah, he is a
beauty ! "

" But the young lady ? "

" Yes, sir, yes. Such a horse ! such a
horse ! "

" When and how can I see her ? "

" When you please, and where you like."

" Alone ? "

" No ; Don Lucas himself will show it."

" It ? Idiot ! "

" The horse ! the horse ! "

The more Frank pressed for specific news of Lola, the more Pepe prevaricated and begged the question. So Frank was glad to go out to Agua Dulce in person, to try his luck for himself.

At the time fixed, he rode to the farm, Pepe behind him. Lucas and Alejandro met them a little beyond the farm buildings, and as they interchanged salutations, Pepe whispered to his master—

" That is the horse, the dark chestnut which the *amo* rides. The Bat, *El Murcie-lago*, they call him. Look, Señor; was there ever perfection such as this? See how he steps ; and his tail, it is long and fine as a maiden's hair; and how noble, how amiable is his temper. See, you might ride him with a silver thread."

At this moment Lucas, with the love of

display that is not uncommon among strangers, was performing a few second-hand manège tricks—circling, reversing, caracolling, twisting his horse in and out, as if it were a sort of machine to be shown off by the regular movement of its wheels and working gear.

But although the " Bat " was thus decked out for inspection, as a Circassian slave might be to please a possible purchaser, it was easy to see the horse's good points beneath the nondescript wrappings that marred his beauty. For all the rusty bridle with its dangling tassels of red and yellow worsted, the square Spanish saddle covered by a strip of sheepskin that hung as low as the dirty stirrup-irons, the ribbons that plentifully adorned his mane and tail, Frank knew that this was as good a bit of stuff as he had yet seen in the country; —a low-built horse, clean and firm in the flanks, of great girth, with a splendid crest and beautiful legs. The head, well put on, and perfect of its kind, proved blood, as shape and form altogether gave promise of speed.

There was a good deal of flourish about the

introduction. Lucas launched out in the usual high-strained compliments and assurances of devotion. He was Frank's secure servant to be commanded to the death; all that was in the farm or that Lucas owned in this world was unreservedly and unhesitatingly at Frank's disposal. No one would have been more surprised than Lucas if he had been asked to part even with the end of his cigarette.

Frank replied in due form, and said (which was mere invention) that Don Lucas' reputation had reached him in England as a high-bred *caballero*, whose gentlemanliness was unequalled in Southern Spain.

"And your horses, Señor—I am told they are of surpassing excellence."

"I have a few *potros*, but they are valueless; were it not so I would offer them to you. It would be but an empty compliment to present that which is worthless to a noble Señor of such consideration and merit."

"*Nada*," replied Frank, not to be outdone, "I could not deprive you of your great treasures, and such they are I know well—jewels."

" Diamonds that have mouths, who would buy them? So runs the proverb."

" Will you open the casket and let me see them? If there be many such as that you ride, your stock would be worth more than a sack of withered fruit."

" Yes, it is a pretty beast—pretty, but no more. I ride it mostly myself."

" You would not sell it, then ?"

" Oh no; it is yours for nothing if you wish."

Frank knew what this meant. Between the declaration it was not for sale, its offer as a gift, and the first preposterous price which Don Lucas would fix after many entreaties, there would be very wide intervals, requiring several hours of hard bargaining.

Meanwhile Alejandro had ranged up along-side the servant, and sought with natural inquisitiveness to pump him. Pepe was not averse to being cross-questioned; it gave him an opening for enlarging upon the wealth and high qualities of his master, some of which would doubtless illumine also the man with reflected light.

Was Frank rich? Yes, as the Archbishop of Toledo. Of high lineage? His relatives were of the bluest blood in London; and owned there a palace which covered more acres than the Escorïal. In what did he chiefly occupy himself? In travel and the chase of fierce beasts; he had a magazine of weapons, such as would shame the Royal Armoury at Madrid. But when Pepe, pressed hard, confessed that Frank was a subaltern in one of the regiments that garrisoned the Rock, Alejandro lost some of the transcendent respect which he was at first disposed to bestow upon the splendid stranger. To Alejandro's mind there was an utter inability to connect anything superb with the position of a simple soldier lieutenant, such as he was himself. Spanish subalterns live' on a pittance that forbids much outlay beyond shirt-cuffs and wax for their moustachios.

And so they rode on. Lucas had told Frank that, in expectation of his visit, a few colts had been brought in from the pastures where they grazed to the *corral* of the farm, and here they waited the English gentleman's

disposal. This, to Frank's delight, meant the
entire run to the house. Surely he must meet
Lola now. As they got nearer the house the
path narrowed—it was a mere track at best—
and crossed a grip full of stagnant water.
Lucas had ridden on ahead, and Frank, who
followed, to avoid a muddy, slushy crossing,
put his horse at the open drain, and hopped
over it like a bird. Alejandro was in ectasies.

" The gentleman is in the cavalry ? " he
said. " No ? Not in the cavalry, but in the
military service surely ? "

Frank said he was an infantry officer.

" And you can ride like that ! But you
learnt in the hippodromo—in the riding-school,
of course ! No ? It is a marvel—a marvel
unequalled since Adam sinned. Ah ! " he
added, anxious to do something for the credit
of his native land, slighted, as it were, by
the horsemanship of this stranger, " but you
should have seen Juan Picador de los Rios of
the Seventh Castillejos regiment of horse—
what a rider was there ! Along the streets,
over the wide plains, and jumps and races of
horse-jockies—pouf ! Señor, he was the de-

light of all Spain. Ah! if you had but known
Juan."

Frank regretted that he had not been so far
fortunate.

After this Alejandro asked many questions,
turning all of them upon the military profession. His uniform, why did not Frank wear
it? It was not usual, Frank said, upon a
journey, or indeed at all, except when really
performing duty. Alejandro was astonished.

"I never take mine off. I am always thus,
clothed and ready, my sword by my side, and
revolver loaded. I could take the field, if need
were, now, at this very instant."

Frank, not well up in Spanish politics, was
somewhat surprised, wondering what foes were
dreaded. Was invasion an hourly bugbear in
Spain, as it sometimes is in our own " highly
favoured " land ?

Alejandro explained that matters were
somewhat ticklish up above—at Madrid, that
is to say; and at any moment he, Alejandro
Peñaflor, might be called to contribute towards
the overthrow of an insurrection, or the ele-
vation of a new dynasty.

"And you wear for gala-dress a coat of red ? " he went on.

"Yes; red is our colour."

"Ah! so I have heard. There were some few of your troops here, I think, in our War of Independence, when we drove Napoleon out of Spain ? "

Frank replied that he believed a tradition to that effect existed, and that an English general, Wellington, was much mixed up in the affair.

"His name I do not remember to have heard—he is not mentioned in our histories. But there were some English soldiers here I know—and Portuguese ; my grandfather saw them. He was with Castaños in the Pyrenees."

History perhaps credits the British with a little more active contribution to the results gained in the Peninsular War.

But now they were at the Cortijo, and the stud was already drawn up for inspection in the inner yard. One or two farm-helpers were about, to bring up horse after horse, over each of which Lucas expatiated with a stream of eulogy worthy a better object. Frank listened with patience; he was in no hurry to conclude the bargain, for every minute gained brought him nearer the chance of meeting Lola. But every horse was seen, and as yet he got no sign. So he bought one, a stout, strong, cob-like horse, that would do for the winter's hunting, and began to question Lucas about the Bat.

The horse was not for sale. Nothing would induce his owner to part with him. Frank persisted, but Lucas said the horse was too great a treasure. He was of the purest blood; the Sultan of Morocco had no better in all his stables. Indeed, he was bred from a barb in the Queen's stables, which she had received straight from the Moorish Court, and his dam was a mare of Cordova, owned by Don Francisco Gutierrez Gonsalvo de Cordova, lineal heir to the "Great Captain" himself. "This horse," said Lucas, "was very dear to him." "And would be to me," thought Frank, when, by and by, Lucas, pressed hard, said he would take seventy-five ounces for him — seventy-five *onzas*, doubloons, royal

pieces of gold, each as big as a warming-
pan.

The sum meant about £250 English, and
was a preposterous price.

" I will not deprive you of your treasure,"
said Frank. " Money is not yet a drug where
I come from, and for seventy-five doubloons
I might buy an elephant."

Spaniards cannot understand " chaff."

" If the Señor wants an elephant, there
will be one here with the show next week.
I thought he was a *caballero*, a *horseman*,"
replied Lucas, looking black.

Frank had no notion of being put down,
but although an angry answer rose to his
lips, he said nothing, but going towards his
horse, quietly remounted and prepared to
leave the place. Alejandro came forward to
shake hands and say good-bye. " Till we
meet again," said Frank ; then waving a short
farewell to Lucas, who bade him God-speed,
after the manner of the country, Frank Wriottesley rode away.

But as he went out under the great gateway, he by chance looked back and saw up

above, at a window, thrust through the lattice, a little hand which held a fan and waved, as it were, both recognition and adieu.

Lucas, left to himself, was furious at the chance he had lost. Nor did Pepe, who lingered behind to take charge of Frank's other purchase, soothe him much with the first words he spoke.

"You opened your mouth too wide, Señor Don Lucas."

"Too wide, *tunante* (rascal) ? How can one swallow a big morsel else ? I saw the Englishman liked the horse. It fitted his eye. If he wants it he must pay the price."

"Not that price; it is too much."

"Is the horse mine or yours, *pillo* (thief) ? Stick not your spoon into my broth."

"My master is not a fool. He knows a horse from a haystack."

"Nor am I a fool—more than God has made me; not so far as men would wish me to be. I am not the man to tune bagpipes— I like to play my own music. I know how many turns a key makes."

"When cakes are scarce, brown bread should

suffice," said Pepe sententiously. "If you can't get your own price, you'll have to take his."

"Neither his price will I admit, nor your hairy tongue. You have more talk than an attorney, and I less patience. *Anda,* hook it, or I shall treat you to a yard or two of stick."

Whereat Pepe in alarm quickly retreated. But he was hardly gone before Lucas repented him of his hastiness. He had no real desire to close the transaction, knowing perfectly that with half the price demanded he would be right well paid for the Bat. It was his native rapacity and greed which had tempted him to demand the seventy-five doubloons; and now that he saw how completely he had failed, he was willing enough to forego a part of his exorbitant profit. The question was how to reopen communications with Frank. After much thought, he resolved to send Miguel into the town to make overtures of peace.

"Shall we go also?" asked Ramona of Lola when alone with her after dinner.

"And why?"

" You did not see him—the *rubio*—the English youth. I did, and he me. He looked up as he rode away ; I waved my fan, and he kissed his hand. I would gladly meet him again."

Lola was puzzled. Did Ramona know more than she pretended ? Had she recognised in Frank Wriottesley the officer they had met in the Fair, or was she only eager to strike up an acquaintance with a stranger whose appearance pleased her ? Then came a flash of jealousy. What if Ramona and Frank understood each other ? What if they were old friends already ? A cold chill struck her, and for the moment she was utterly miserable.

" Well, what say you ? " went on Ramona, pressing for an answer.

" It would be unmaidenly." Lola was struggling with herself. She was anxious, very anxious, to speak to Frank Wriottesley again ; but to go thus in search of him ! Her maiden modesty shuddered at the bare thought. " Besides," she went on, " Doña Teresa would not suffer it."

" Madam my mother would never know.

We should go to Ximena to buy stores—
there is much that we require from the
town."

"It will be so deceitful."

"Oh, pigeon without gall! you are too sen-
sitive to live."

"My grandfather—your mother, if she discovered—would they not be enraged ? "

"Were they never young themselves, that
they would deny us the sunlight wherein to
flap our wings ?   Ours is the season for
noviaje, for lovemaking. Old age creeps on
fast enough ; *el muerto al hoyo, y el vivo al
bollo*, the dead to the grave, the living to eat
cake. Let us make the most of our time.
But why waste words ? If you will not come,
then will I go alone."

This was worse than ever. How could
Lola suffer Ramona out of her sight ?

"I like these *rubios*—as you do, *hija*, I
think, unless you have forgotten already yonder
light-haired foreigner that we met at the Fair.
Have you then found some other lover ? A
rey muerto rey puesto—One king dead, the
next king crowned."

Lola was terribly perplexed. On one side, her sense of propriety restrained her, on the other she was egged onward by a strange fear lest Ramona should supplant her. For some time she vacillated. Was it strange that in the end she gave in ? To remain behind would be to surrender all her hopes—hopes now nascent and newly fledged since Pepe had come calling himself Frank's ambassador, and proving that this English officer still bore her in mind.

Lucas, by way of encouragement, had described Frank to Miguel as a fierce-tempered, crossgrained brute, who would give him "*muy mal rato*," a very bad time. The little man was delighted therefore to find in Wriottesley an old acquaintance.

Their business was soon concluded; Frank offered fifty doubloons readily enough for the Bat, on certain conditions, which Miguel was to convey to his brother. After which Miguel said—

"I must now return to the ladies—my sister and Dolorcita—the little cousin to whom you were so kind, Señor Englishman ;

they await me at the house of a friend in
the lower town."

"I should be glad to renew my acquaintance," said Frank eagerly, adding, without
waiting for permission, "I will accompany
you."

Miguel was not over-pleased, yet he could
not refuse.   There was every reason for
keeping on good terms with Frank, at least
until the sale of the Bat was completed.
Any failure in the negotiations Lucas would
certainly visit upon his little brother.

Ramona and Lola had left the house before
the others arrived, and were seated on a
bench under the trees that· margined a
narrow strip of gravel path, and which
passed in Ximena for the Alameda or public
walk of the town.

Frank bowed to Ramona, and held out
his hand to Lola, who, blushing vividly,
said, "How do do?" in her broken English,
but with her eyes fixed upon the ground.

Ramona, seeing her mistake, was at first
disposed to be annoyed.   On a closer view
she readily recognised Frank Wriottesley,

and remembered him as the man who had paid her cousin so much attention at the Casino Ball. Yet it was clear that this meeting had been none of Lola's making, and after a short struggle Ramona forgave her.

Frank had laid himself, figuratively, at the feet of the ladies, with an offer to kiss their shoes, which act of homage gave him rank at once as a high bred *caballero*.

" How well you speak our language," said Ramona. " Since when have you learnt it ? "

"Since I was at San Roque. I had strong reasons for wishing to know, it."

" A marvel ! to learn Castilian in a few short months, and speak it now as only the *Madrileños* can ! " cried Ramona.

Lola said nothing. She was wondering whether she knew the real reason which had induced Frank Wriottesley to study Spanish.

" I wished to travel, to become thoroughly acquainted with Spain, to learn all your manners and customs."

" And you have done so ? " asked Miguel.

"I have visited the chief cities, Seville, Granada, Malaga, Cadiz."

" And yet you waste time in this wretched corner! Surely some great attraction must have led you hither?" went on Ramona, looking mischievously at Lola.

" Possibly," replied Frank.

" To ask what would, perhaps, be indiscreet," said Ramona.

" The secret is not my own. Besides, I think I was mistaken, and I begin to wish I had stayed away."

Lola had listened in silence but with a beating heart. There was no mistaking Frank's meaning, however, as he spoke the last words; but what could she say? only the merest commonplace.

" It grows late; we should be returning;" and Frank, like most men, blind to the real state of affairs, began to be very down-hearted and discouraged.

" *Anda!* Dolorcita of my heart," whispered Ramona, "you do not deserve a *novio*. Have you no tongue? no words of welcome for this youth who has come so far to see you? Leave him then to me!"

" *Bien* (well), as you please. Come,

Miguel," said Lola briskly, "*a casa :* home!"
and with that she rose and walked quickly
away.

Some one followed her as fast. Not Miguel,
but Frank, who said when he had caught
her up—

" You are not angry, Señorita ? "

" Oh no ! why should I be ? "

" I had looked forward so much to meeting you again."

" Yes ? "

" And you ? "

" I had almost forgotten." She was picking to pieces the flower she had carried in
her waistband.

" You left San Roque so suddenly. I
went back "——

" I saw you riding out with an English
lady, fair and beautiful as a star."

" The wife of a brother officer. Her husband rode with us also. Did you not see
him ? "

" Tell me," said Lola without heeding his
question, " Englishwomen are all *rubias*,
light-haired and white like she is ? " and as

she spoke for the first time she raised her eyes and looked at him.

"Some are red as carrots, others black as sloes. There are few who can compare with the beauties of Southern Spain. They have not eyes which pierce like flames."

"You have learnt then to flatter, Señor Don "——

"Francisco!" and she repeated the name.

"And you, *Señorita*, what is your *gracia?*"

"Dolores!" in a low voice.

"No more?"

"My friends call me Lola, sometimes Lolita."

"And may I?"

"Are you a friend, Don Francisco? I have only seen you once before, and that was long, long ago. It is many months since the Fair."

"It will not be fault of mine if we do not meet soon again. Do you remain here long?"

"Probably not. My grandfather wishes me to return to Gibraltar before the winter."

"There are others there perhaps who wish the same."

"No, Señor, I have no *novios*."

"Then the young fellows there have no eyes?"

"I have seen none amongst them," cried Lola with great disdain, "that I would care to favour."

"You are hard to please."

"*Los gustos son como panderos*—Tastes are like tambourines, not all alike."

"I shall know when you return to the Rock."

"How?"

"Josefa! I took Pepe as groom only to oblige her."

"Perhaps I shall tell my grandfather, and I shall get a new dueña."

"No matter; I should find you, as I have just now. But I have had to hunt long both high and low. Who would have guessed that you were hidden here like a grain of gold among a heap of rocks?"

"Those knew who had a right to know," said Lola, coquettishly.

" And I am not one ? Some day you will talk differently perhaps."

" When, then ? "

" By and by ! "

" Those who start along By-and-by Street reach some day to 'Never' Square."

" Never is a long day; yet I wish we might never reach the Cortijo, which is now so near."

They were still some distance ahead of Miguel and Ramona, and were entering the narrow lane margined by a hedge of aloes and prickly pears which led straight to the farm.

" Tell me, Don Francisco," said Lola suddenly; " you said you had reasons for learning Spanish. What were they ? "

" I will tell you on one condition. Do you agree ? "

" *A ver !* Let us see."

" Will you tell me whether there is a *reja* at Agua Dulce ? "

Lola looked down with flushed cheeks. Frank's question meant that he wished to prosecute his suit in the true Spanish fashion, coming after dark with guitar in hand, shrouded in a long cloak, to exchange soft whispers through the iron bars with the girl of his heart.

"You go on too fast, Don Francisco," said Lola at length.

"May I hope?"

"Such idle hopes are like thistles—fit only for donkeys' food."

"Then must I go back as I have come? *Adios*, Señorita. My pains then were wasted. You know I learnt Spanish "——

"Yes?"

"Only to talk to you."

A crimson blush rose to our heroine's cheek, but it was one of pleasure and delight. She did not pause to consider whether this bold statement of Frank's would bear the test of inquiry, but accepted it as a sort of clenching argument in proof of the truth of his attachment. She felt she had found her mate, and with childlike trustfulness, her heart straightway went out to this man, and she loved him, as she thought, at once and for ever.

Soon after this came adieus. The ladies entered the house, while Frank with Miguel went in search of Lucas, who was somewhere about the farm. A short colloquy followed. Frank was ready to give fifty doubloons for the Bat, but wished first to try him; and as Lucas peremptorily refused to send the horse into the Rock, it was arranged that Frank should return another day with a friend, and then give a final answer.

He saw nothing more of Lola that night, although he lingered about the house long after nightfall. There were several windows opening to the front, but not a sign of life in any of them. After all, Lola had made no promise to appear, and Frank, if somewhat disappointed, found that his respect for her was increased by her reluctance to meet him thus clandestinely at the *reja* after dark.

CHAPTER XI.

THE BAT.

NEXT day Frank returned to Gibraltar in search of Sproule. He wanted his advice about the Bat.

"All right, my pippin!" cried Sproule. "I'm with you. If he's what you describe, he'll help us to spoil the Egyptians."

It was agreed that they should ride out together, taking with them Mountebank, an old English "plater," which Sproule had brought out with him to Gibraltar as a little turf speculation, but which had not been as yet of much use to him. Now he might give them a line as to the Bat's real speed.

But Mrs Sproule, when, as in duty bound, the scheme was propounded to her, protested against being left out of it.

" After all I've done for you, Mr Wriottesley, I do call it shabby."

" But it's a forty-mile ride."

" As if I couldn't ride forty miles ! "

" We know you could, my precious ! " said
Sproule ; " but we thought of spending the
night at Ximena. The pace will be a trifle
fast, perhaps, at the trial, and the horses had
better rest a little before we bring them back
to the Rock."

" All the better. I should like to see
something of the place."

" You'd never be able to stand it," went
on Frank.

" Isn't there an hotel ? "

Frank laughed aloud.

" There's a *posada*, where the sitting-room
is in the stable, and the best bedroom has
no windows."

" It won't matter for one night. Besides,
those Spanish people will perhaps put us
up."

Frank did not think this very probable.
Hospitality to this extent is not much practised, as he knew, in Southern Spain. But

he could not talk Mrs Sproule out of her desire to go to Ximena, and accordingly the trio started one bright October morning for Spain. Cantering gaily across the grass upon the Neutral Ground, they soon reached the sentries at the Spanish Lines. Here at once Mrs Sproule got into trouble. A brace of *carabineros*, or custom-house officials, came up as soon as they touched Spanish soil, and insisted upon examining our travellers' luggage. They had none of them more than they carried upon their horses, in wallets and saddle-bags—all toilette necessaries and wearing apparel—nothing more. This Mrs Sproule declared loudly, and in the purest English, but all to no purpose. The more she protested, the more suspicious became the searchers. One man held her horse by the head while the other, firm in the execution of his duty, rifled her wallets. All went on peaceably enough for a time, till at length the searcher came across a piece of scented soap. He was puzzled. With soap in any shape he was but slightly acquainted; stuff of this sort was something entirely new and sur-

prising.   He smelt it, tasted it, chewed it,
and eventually put it into his pocket.   The
unknown and mysterious article was unmistakably contraband.

"The ruffian!   He has stolen my soap,"
cried Mrs Sproule in an angry voice, pointing
at the man with her whip.   "Mr Wriottesley,
do come and help me."

But Frank was also in the hands of the
tormentors, and Mrs Sproule, forgetting herself, struck the *carabinero* smartly on the
hand.   For this she was immediately taken
into custody.   At the cry of *socorro* (help),
an armed escort came out of the guardhouse
hard by, and Mrs Sproule was led off, looking rather white, between two small sentries,
whose fixed bayonets reached rather danger-
ously to within an inch or two of her nose.

Sproule went to his wife's assistance, but
as he could speak no word of Spanish except
"*perdony*," which none of the officials would
accept as an apology, they captured and
removed him also as an accomplice or acces-
sory after the fact.   Had not Frank inter-
fered they would both have incontinently

found their way to the *calabozo*, or dungeon, by which grand name was dignified the one small cell or lock-up attached to the guard-house. Fortunately he had a slight acquaintance with the Spanish Colonel who was commandant at the Lines, and after some demur and the payment of a fine, the two culprits were released.

Mrs Sproule's indignation was too deep-seated to find vent in words. She rode on sulkily, and almost silent, except for a few short and very snappish monosyllables when addressed by her husband or Frank.

Presently they reached the open beach, where their only road led along the narrow strip of good hard sand used by all passengers, whether mounted or on foot. The path, generally much frequented, was to-day quite crowded. There were women carrying enormous baskets full of clothes, clean or dirty, poised marvellously on their heads; droves of donkies laden with charcoal; horses nearly lost to view under cargoes of chopped straw, destined to fill other stomachs than their own; children at play; long lines of fishermen drawing in their nets. Considerate people riding in among the throng would naturally rein in their horses to the slowest pace. Not so Mrs Sproule. Directly she found herself in the open, she gave her steed the whip and galloped forward, seeking perhaps in rapid motion a relief to the fit of bad temper by which she was oppressed. Being an excellent horsewoman, the faster she travelled the better she was pleased. Had there been a fair field before her it would have mattered little now; but no sooner had her horse extended himself than she came plump into the middle of the crowd. To many of the poor wayfarers, trudging painfully along under their burthens, the sound of galloping hoofs coming from behind had a very terrifying effect, and some turned off at once for safety into the heavy sand alongside the road, while others, who paused to look round, were lost. Equally perplexed were those who, facing her, found her riding furiously towards them. In a few short seconds all were scattered to the four winds of heaven.

Pursued now by yells and execrations, Mrs Sproule continued her reckless course, meeting next in full career a string of patient mules laden with heavy stones from the Carnicero quarries, and these, overpowered also with dread, doubtful what to do, dashed some of them into the waves, while not a few turned tail and fled before her, leaving their outraged owners to join in the general cry for revenge upon Mrs Sproule.

The commotion was now at its height. In front raced the English lady, with hair and habit streaming in the wind; behind came a mixed crowd of furious natives of all sexes, shouting, threatening, cursing, seeking the nearest missiles available to cast at their retreating foe. Happily this was a sandy and not a pebbly shore, or the fate of Saint Stephen might have overtaken Mrs Sproule; and the worst that befel her was a slight blow upon the shoulder from a passing loaf, which one infuriated sufferer, regardless of his dinner, had hurled at her as she sped away.

Sproule and Frank were not a little exercised in spirit.

"She'll do some mischief yet!" said the husband as stoically as he could.

"Is he off with her?" asked Frank; adding in an excited voice, "Come on! come on!"

"Not if I know it. No connection with the house over the way. They look wicked these chaps, and I don't want them to think Janita belongs to us. Leave her alone; she knows what's what. She'll sit fast enough. It's not for her I funk."

"There goes another man knocked over!"

"Gad! they're like ninepins."

"The rope! the rope!" interrupted Frank nervously.

All at once he noticed that Mrs Sproule was rapidly approaching the long line of fishermen in single file, who, like an interminable procession, were walking inland, and hauling on the rope that was bringing their nets to shore. Sproule was roused by this.

"She does not see it! She can't pull him in—not at that pace. Hold hard! hold hard!" he shouted. "The rope! the rope!"

In breathless suspense both waited.

"She's down, as I'm a sinner! No! no!

well sat! well sat!" cried Sproule with enthusiasm, as his wife seemingly for a moment blundered, then touched · her horse with the whip; lifted him as it were by the head, and bounded lightly over the half-invisible obstacle.

She was safe. In front the beach was open and free from traffic, and she might continue her Mazeppa-like career for another mile or more without either let or hindrance.

By and by she pulled up her horse to a walk, and then the gentlemen overtook her. They had had no little difficulty in winning their way through the scowling natives, many of whom seemed ready to make violent reprisals. Mrs Sproule's ears should have tingled at the epithets and anathemas hurled at her peccant person; but she had escaped, and her cavaliers, themselves innocent of wrong-doing, could not well be detained. Again Frank came to the rescue, and with handfuls of cigarettes, shoals of coppers, and many soothing words, paved the way to peace. But he lost no time in taking Mrs Sproule to task for her conduct.

"Why didn't they get out of my road?"
she said petulantly, with all the selfishness
of an ill-tempered woman.

"They were on their own road," Frank
replied gravely.

"Well, why didn't they keep their own
side?"

"You know there is no side-path."

"I know that you always take people's
parts against me—and these people, too!
You're much too fond of them; they're not
worth it."

"Your life wouldn't have been worth
much, Mrs Sproule, if I hadn't pacified them.
Lucky I could speak their language a little."

"I see no great advantage in it, and it's
very bad for them. If you didn't encourage
them by talking their own gibberish, perhaps
they'd try to learn English."

A delightful piece of intolerance this, at
which both Sproule and Frank laughed
heartily.

So far they had not prospered much, and
they were doomed to yet greater misfortunes.

Although when they started the weather

was brilliantly bright and fine, as the morning wore on came proof of the Spanish proverb that "the sun which is hot too early never lasts throughout the day." The season, too, was already advanced. To the summer with its stinging heats had succeeded autumn, and now in early October the rains—heavy rains, occasionally almost tropical—for which the soil, parched up and shrivelled by the scorching sun-light and drought, thirsted in numberless wide-mouthed gaps and fissures, were hourly expected. Eyes more experienced than Frank's might have gathered caution at sight of the heavy clouds banking up about mid-day away over the African hills; but · he was blind to the signs of the weather. Since their arrival, months before, they had had no drop of rain. Long disuse breeds in us forgetfulness. It seemed to Frank quite possible that it would never rain again. No dread of wet jackets had ever entered the minds of our travellers; they came entirely unprepared, without waterproofs, without even a complete change of clothes.

The sky was slightly overcast when they

halted at Long Stables to bait and have lunch ;
but hereabouts the cork-trees gather thick,
and there was no view of the distant horizon,
no knowledge that the dark masses of vapour,
which an hour before had seemed so distant
on the hills beyond the Straits, were reaching
rapidly upwards, promising soon to obscure
the very zenith with their ominous pall. All
round, the air was still ; there reigned abroad
a peaceful but expectant .calm, as if Nature
with folded . hands waited contentedly and
in happy silence for the refreshing, revivifying
showers, long delayed, but now at . last
unmistakably at hand.

Our .party was again in the saddle and a
mile or two on the road when the first few
raindrops fell. By the time they emerged
from the corkwood and reached the open
plain, it was raining heavily. The prospect
was chill and drear.

"I don't like the look of it at all," said
Frank gloomily.

"Nor I," Sproule added. "We're in for a
Snorter."

"Is it much farther ?" asked Mrs Sproule,

involuntarily shaking her shoulders together with a sort of shudder.

" Eight or ten miles to the Cortijo. We shall be drenched."

No doubt. The downpour was now search-ing and persistent. The raindrops fell like small-shot, under which the horses winced at every stroke, as did their riders when now and again the driving sleet touched them on face or neck or hands. Soon all the narrow roadside ruts and channels were filled with water ; the half-dried river was fast swelling to a raging torrent ; the ground underfoot grew boggy and insecure.

Sliding, slipping, muddy, bedraggled, a miserable crew, the three travellers pushed on. Yet Mrs Sproule bore up bravely enough ; it was her own wish which had brought her to this, and sooner than confess herself in the wrong she would have endured total immer-sion, perhaps drowning itself. Sproule's coat was thick, and his constitution, like his con-science, tough. Although he was now satu-rated to the skin, he uttered no word of com-plaint, taking his wetting as he might accept

a clod of clay in his eye when riding a flat
race and lagging some way behind. Frank,
who was also soaking wet, thought less of
himself than of the others. He felt that he
had brought them to this, and wished he
could see an end to the trouble.

The nearest dwelling was the Cortijo.
Frank was not indisposed to halt there and
claim hospitality for the night. Yet to these
people he was nearly a stranger, and they
might fairly remind him that a mile further
on rest and shelter could be obtained by those
who cared to pay the charges of the *posada*,
a poor country-inn of Ximena town. But
Frank knew this to be a mere den of a place,
an unsavoury, insect-infested, squalid hole,
the discomforts of which, even under ordinary
circumstances, would be trying to so fastidious
a lady as Mrs Sproule. Just now they would
probably prove quite insupportable. The ways
of the denizens at Agua Dulce were probably
primitive, but at least Mrs Sproule would find
cleanliness, dry clothes, and some show of
sympathy—none of which could be counted
upon at the *posada*. For her sake, therefore,

he resolved to stop at the farm, and use all his eloquence to persuade them to take her in.

But in truth Mrs Sproule's appearance should have been more eloquent than any words of his. Poor woman! as she sat doubled up on her saddle, disconsolate and shivering, she ought to have moved to compassion the flintiest heart. Her habit seemed of blotting paper, so thirstily had it sucked up all the moisture of the air; her collar, once so well starched and prim, was now limp and nearly liquid; her pale locks, escaping many of them from her once even and trimly arranged plaits, hung down straight like hanks of moistened tow.

In answer to the deep-toned gate-bell came first a girl who helped in the kitchen, then Miguel, then Lucas, both of whom, recognising in Frank the probable purchaser of the Bat, were profuse in their commiseration and offers of assistance. The house and all it contained was of course at the disposal of the travellers; it was theirs—let them but issue their commands.

Frank translated this kindly speech very literally for the benefit of Mrs Sproule.

" They are very good," she gasped out, taking it for granted that the Spaniards meant all they said.

" A warm fire, some dry clothes, and a cup of tea will soon put me to rights ; " and she prepared to dismount from her horse.

" Is the lady ill ? Does she wish to enter the house ? " asked Lucas, evidently surprised.

" She is nearly dead with fatigue, wet also to the skin. Will not madam your mother take compassion on her, and entertain her—at least for this one night ? "

Lucas shrugged his shoulders.

" What is the delay ? " asked Mrs Sproule petulantly. " Really, Mr Wriottesley, I think you might be more considerate. You seem to ignore the fact that I am benumbed and nearly dead with wet and cold."

" It is not my fault. These people are not to be hurried." Then turning to Lucas— " Surely you cannot turn from your doors to-night a lady in such a plight as this ? "

" I will ask my mother; she rules here, not I," replied Lucas in a doubtful voice.

"Oh, rot it all !" put in Sproule. "Don't let us be beholden to the brutes. You're not dead-beat yet, Janita, are you ? Let's go on to the hotel."

" I tell you there isn't one," said Frank quite crossly.

" I'd rather go back to Gibraltar," groaned Mrs Sproule.

" That's impossible; it's too late. You'd have to spend the night at the Lines."

But now Lucas returned, and with him the two girls, Ramona and Lola. To both of them Frank bowed—a short sort of salutation, but there was a bright light in his eye when it fell upon the face of our heroine, and something more than mere gratitude in his tones when he thanked Lola for her kindness, when, acting as spokeswoman, she came forward, and in her pretty broken English begged Mrs Sproule to descend.

Inside there had been a short fight. Doña Teresa at first stoutly resisted the invasion, declaring that her house was no hostelry, and

that she was aghast at the want of manners
of these English in thrusting themselves forward upon strangers, and into places to which
they were never invited.   Lola combated these
arguments with a warmth that would certainly
have roused anger in Doña Teresa, were it
not that Don Mariano's granddaughter was a
privileged person, to be treated always with a
certain respect.   Ramona said little, but she
half guessed the real truth, that Lola was thus
anxious on behalf of these English folk because
they were in some way connected with this
new lover who dwelt on the Rock.   Of course,
the exact state of the case was plain to her
when she came out with Lola to the door,
and with some thoughtfulness she at once
took charge of Mrs Sproule, leading her
with her husband into the house, while Frank
and Lola were for the moment left alone
together.

"You have a kind heart, Señorita.   This
poor lady needs all your help."

"We are not as savage as the heathen blacks,
Mr Englishman, although we live, perhaps, in
an obscure, benighted spot."

" Where you are, Señorita, is for me the centre of the world."

"*Anda!*" (Go to!) cried Lola. " I had hoped you were too wise to use such flattering words."

" Shall I see you to-morrow when we come out to try the horse ? "

" I know not."

" And you do not care ? "

Lola did not answer.

" When do you return to the Rock ? "

" Next week, I hope."

" You wish it, then ? "

" Oh yes ! "

" Why ? "

" Is it not my real home—where my grandfather resides, where I myself was born, where I have many friends ? It is but natural that I should be glad to see it again."

Frank would have pressed her to tell him whether there was not just now one reason more why she should prefer to go back to her grandfather's house, but at this moment Sproule came out, and the lovers hastily parted.

" She'll be as right as ninepence there," said

Sproule. "They'll get her to bed by and by, and make her snug. She wanted me to stop, but I'm drenched too, and I can't well leave the horses till they're comfortably housed."

"Certainly the horses should be your first care," cried Frank, amused at their relative importance with Sproule's wife.

"Well, you know, I can't do much for Janita. Besides, these people won't want more of us than can be helped messing about. I say, Master Frank, that's a bright-eyed ' snorer' " —this was his joking version of Señora—"you had in tow. You seem pretty thick, too."

"Perhaps we'd better push on," replied Frank in a hurry.

"All right, my hearty. A nod's as good as a wink, you know. We'll toddle on. Janita's in good hands."

They certainly did their best to make Mrs Sproule comfortable at the farm, thanks chiefly to the energy with which Lola acquitted herself of the charge laid upon her by Frank Wriottesley. She insisted upon giving up her own room; she herself acted as maid, and with deft fingers relieved Mrs Sproule of her dripping habit. She it was who searched out among her own rather scanty wardrobe garments of all sorts—not quite a fit, perhaps, for Lola was the taller of the two, and though slender, not of so slight a figure as Mrs Sproule; yet were they dry and warm, and clean as so many new pins. It was Lola who busied herself to prepare some refreshment suited to an English lady's taste. Mrs Sproule had clamoured loudly for tea, but there was not a single leaf in the house. The fragrant herb is counted rather as a medicine in these outlandish parts, going frequently by the name of "fever water," a decoction good for *calenturas*, a bitter unpleasant medicinal draught, allied to the bark of the *quina quina*, which ages ago the good Jesuit fathers had brought from the New World. Doña Teresa was indeed both frightened and indignant when she heard of Mrs Sproule's request, protesting loudly that beyond question this guest whom she had so unwillingly admitted into her house was suffering from some contagious disorder, from which it was fated for them one and all to die. The cook was equally puzzled, and wondered much how this tea-water was prepared. Was it boiled with tomatoe-sauce to give it a flavour, or did the English make it into a soup with green pepper and olive-oil ?

Mrs Sproule received all these attentions with calm condescension, as if they were her undoubted right. Grateful acknowledgment of favours received was not an active virtue of hers, nor did the memory of what she owed these kind Samaritans debar her from speaking afterwards in the most contemptuous and disparaging terms of the night she had spent in this Spanish country-house. She abused the accommodation in no measured terms, describing in graphic language the interior of the farm, its bare unfurnished rooms, the terrible character of the food they provided for her, the garlic obtrusive in every dish, the rancid oil of which the salad was made, the olives which every one tore to pieces with their fingers or teeth. Nor was she more charitable towards the ladies, least of all to Lola, whose unwearied kindness had really laid her under the heaviest obligations. They were all underbred, commonplace people, and Lola particularly, with her great staring eyes and too plentiful hair, could pretend to no good looks, any more than, with her retiring modest ways, she could claim to have the manners of a lady.

All this and more Mrs Sproule poured into Frank's unwilling ears when the gentlemen rejoined her next day. He was, in truth, not sorry when the trial was over, and with it the ill-starred expedition which had given such increased acerbity to Janita's tongue.

CHAPTER XII.

SAVE ME FROM MY FRIENDS.

THERE was now no reason why Lola should remain at Agua Dulce. She had gone thither to be out of harm's way when without a dueña's protection; now that the latter had returned to duty, Lola might also return. Her grandfather's love for her was so great that he could not bear, he said, to be long separated from the child of his heart. Lola herself was ready enough to go back to Gibraltar; that she had not already started was due to the entreaties of her cousins, whose affection was always demonstrative if not deep-seated.

But the attractions that were drawing Lola to the Rock were new and imperious. It was here that Frank Wriottesley lived; here she might meet with him again; or, if fate forbade such good fortune, she might perchance see him from time to time—see him in the far-off distance, a being of another sphere, whom yet she might innocently worship. For—conceal it she could not from herself—his image was now deeply engraved in her heart. Although their acquaintance was still of recent date, she felt that she loved him thoroughly and for ever—as do the eager and impressionable daughters of the South, loving once, and once only, but with a warmth and fervour unknown to the denizens of colder climes. Her love was now part and parcel of her; of rapid growth, no doubt, yet intertwined with and over-arching her existence. It had taken complete possession of her; to struggle against it would be simply futile, a mere waste of labour. Nor was hers the wish. Her affection was returned— of this she was assured, trusting in that respect to the unerring intuition of a maiden's heart. She could read as in a book, in Frank's glad eyes, in the notes of his joyous voice, the love that was altogether hers. At the

moment, she gave herself no thought how
all this might end; consequences, ways and
means, obstacles present or to come, all are
ignored when a girl is consumed by the
ardour of a first attachment.   To be with
Frank, to look upon his face and to listen
to his words, these seemed to constitute now
her only ideas of happiness and pleasure.
She had not the slightest conception how far
a passion of this engrossing character might
carry her; nor had she a friend, least of all
that truest of true friends, a mother, to guide
her with advice and counsel drawn from her
own experience in life.   Happily Lola was
not wanting in ballast; pride would soon
have combined with common sense to fortify
her self-respect, if that indeed were threatened.
Her love, so far, though deep, was innocent
and guileless, it would soon have taken
alarm had Frank, presuming on its intensity,
sought with insidious arguments and false
cozening words to do her wrong.   But
happily, also, Frank Wriottesley was honest
and loyal, a high-souled, true-hearted young
fellow, impetuous, hot-headed, and eager, but

one who would have scorned a base action, and who was actuated now by the thoroughly honourable intention—if he could win this treasure—of making her his wife.

It was not strange that an acquaintance begun under such conditions should make rapid strides. These two young people were both of the same way of thinking, both ardent, both impressionable. No set declaration was needed between them. Each readily recognised the influence exercised by the other; both seemed satisfied, without the aid of explicit language, of the feelings they mutually entertained. Lola had accepted Frank's love quite as a matter of course; it made no difference that he had not stated it in so many words; it was hers she knew. Little less certain was Frank, even without confession, that she returned his affection without hesitation, wholly and truly, almost from the first.

But just as this love was intense, so was it unreflective. They were a foolish pair these two, and did many silly things, quite without a thought. An English Mrs Grundy

might have been a trifle shocked at the manner.
in which Frank pursued his suit. She 'would
have held up her hands in horror at the notion
of an unmarried girl meeting an unknown
lover clandestinely without the consent of her
friends. My precise and demure readers will
doubtless hear with regret that Lola came
day after day with Josefa to seat herself about
noon just below the statue of General Elliot,
in the gardens of the Alameda, and that there,
quite by accident of course, they found a young
gentleman, seemingly without any occupation
in life but that of waiting to receive them.
It was dreadfully wrong, too, that Josefa
should suffer Lola, after the first greetings, to
wander amid the shady walks, round and
round the garden plots, or in among the
embrasures of the carefully concealed battery
placed near, and known familiarly as "the Snake
in the Grass." Frank Wriottesley was much
to blame, again, for making interest to be
posted always at the New Mole when it
came to his turn to mount guard; and there
was no reason on earth why he should waste
so many hours in visiting his sentries, par-

ticularly those stationed round about Rosia; still less was he called upon to linger for half-an-hour at a time near a certain cottage which it was no part of his duty to guard. They were all to blame—Frank for proposing, Lola for consenting, most of all Josefa for betraying her sacred trust and in encouraging these dreadful doings.

But in truth the offence which our lovers committed was more against the letter than the spirit of propriety. Their sole desire in this, the first flush of their attachment, was to meet, and to meet as often as they could. The hours apart were the longest and the dreariest of the twenty-four, and to reduce them to the lowest was the great aim and object of their lives. Lola herself had as yet no notion she was doing wrong; it was thus that flirtations were carried on by other girls of her class, and she was but following the custom of the land of her birth. No one had ever explained to her that the only proper and blameless method of encouraging a young man's attentions was to meet him at the skating rink, or to dance and sit out with him

for hours at a ball, to ride with him next day
in the Park, to spend weeks together in
country-houses or on board yachts, to have
almost unlimited opportunities of being in his
society without even a whispered complaint
from the impassive lookers on. Lola had
never heard of these fashionable methods
by which love-making is rendered easy in
the great world, nor if she had, were they
within her reach. She could but continue
simply and in perfect good faith as she had
begun, contented to drift happily down the
stream, hand in hand with the man of her
choice. Her conscience was easy, just as
her mind was pure and without a stain.

It cannot be said, however, that the other
parties to this peculiar love-suit were altogether as happy in their minds. Matters could
not go on thus for ever. There were times
when Frank Wriottesley remembered that he
was still dependent upon his uncle, Sir Hector
Harrowby, a man of strong temper, as we
know, whose ire might easily be aroused.
How would he receive the news that Frank
proposed to take as his wife—as the future

mistress of Grimswych Park—a nameless girl, a foreigner almost, foreign at least in education and in the tongue she spoke? .When such thoughts arose he grew perturbed in spirit, anxious, doubtful of the future, not varying one whit in his strong affection for Lola, but somewhat sorrowful for her, regretful that fate was so adverse, and that it was not in his power to spare her even the temporary anguish which his uncle might cause if at first he refused his consent to their marriage. But such forebodings were unnatural with such a character as Frank's; he could not be unsanguine long; the moment he met Lola again, all gloomy thoughts vanished into thin air, and he was angry with himself for doubting at all. Who could resist her? he asked with lover-like raptures; and for the time he was again at ease, feeling satisfied that all would come right in the end.

Confident in his own uprightness, Frank could look on ahead and wait thus hopefully. Not so Josefa, who was in a perpetual fever lest affairs might at any moment take an unsatisfactory turn. Her master might discover her double-dealing, and she would forthwith be ejected from his house. Of course she . knew discovery was certain to come sooner or later, but it was naturally her desire to postpone as long as possible the inevitable day. Perhaps she might succeed in shifting the blame from herself, and blinding Don Mariano to the nefarious part she had played. But as this was doubtful, she cast about to indemnify herself otherwise. Hers was a base nature, she could stoop low indeed to serve her own ends. She was ready to sacrifice Lola just as she. had already betrayed her trust to her master, and waited but a hint from Frank to assist him in any infamous plan. Prepared to go to any lengths, even to the extreme wickedness of inducing Lola to leave her home, the more she pondered the more satisfied she became that this, in truth, was the consummation that would suit her personally best. To purchase her complicity Frank would doubtless pay handsomely—pay, as it was clear he could, a large sum, sufficient equivalent for the service rendered. With

SAVE ME FROM MY FRIENDS.

this money she might retire to some sheltered
spot among the Sierras or upon the smiling
slopes of the Mediterranean, to spend the
remainder of her days in idleness and com-
parative .ease. No remorse would have
followed her thither; nor had she in advance
one jot of compunction at the contemplation
of the horrible crime to which she was ready
to give her aid. She never for one moment
doubted that Frank's thoughts were as evil
as her own; and, taking this for granted, she
was at no pains to sound him on the subject.
Her time was rather devoted to undermin-
ing Lola, and seeking insidiously to combat
in advance any scruples which the innocent
child might by and by display.

Josefa's chief fear was lest any unforeseen
accident should precipitate a crisis. If this
could be avoided she might trust to her
own skill and good fortune to turn matters
to her own advantage in the end. The
great difficulty was to keep Don Mariano
in continued ignorance of what was going
on ; to prevent Lola from broaching the subject or falling into a full confession. Several

times had our heroine suggested that it was time to present Frank Wriottesley to her grandfather; it was right that the old man should know him, and receive him openly at his house. Josefa, better versed in the old man's sentiments towards the officer-class, used all her eloquence to combat this notion, and to persuade Lola to postpone the introduction from day to day. The dueña did not dare explain her real reason. Lola had an instinctive dislike to aught that was underhand, and she would have been firm in her refusal to receive Frank's addresses were she sure that her grandfather disapproved.

Meanwhile, in all unconscious innocence, firm in her trust of him, and without a particle of self-upbraiding, she continued to meet her lover, telling herself from day to day that she ought not to conceal the true state of affairs much longer from the grand-father who loved her so well, yet still hesi-tating and hanging back, shrinking with true maiden modesty from exposing to view, even before her nearest relative, this new and beautiful possession which she treasured almost as a sacred gift from heaven.

But the crisis which Josefa dreaded was now indeed close at hand, and it came to pass in this wise.

Winter-time is for the English residents and their friends essentially "the gay season" at Gibraltar, when, the climate is, as a rule, perfection, and there is no lack of the sports which are most dear to English hearts. There is shooting of snipe and cock and red-legged partridge in the neighbouring hills; and no talk of licence, of gamelaws, or pre-serves. For those that care to embark more deeply, Barbary supplies wild boar. The Calpe hounds meet twice a week on Spanish soil, and draw large fields to exasperate the uninitiated tillers of the soil by seemingly reckless contempt for growing wheat. The air is fresh if not exactly keen; the Vermilion Sierra wears at times a coating of snow; now and again a film of ice as thick as a bank-note is found in a pail upon the top of the Rock, and our compatriots call the weather season-able, and nearly persuade themselves it is cold. To those native-born the winter is not so much admired. *Al fresco* life is no longer possible; the bands have ceased to play at night upon the Alameda; to the summer moonlight, yellow and strong as Northern sunshine, have succeeded stormy skies and torrents of rain. For them, sports such as we worship have neither meaning nor attraction; to gallop at break-neck pace over uneven ground would be no diversion; dinner-parties are not for them festivities, shooting a mere wanton destruction of animal life. They love gaiety rather, music, crowded gatherings, chatter, spectacles of every sort. The theatre is especially popular, whether the performance be the music of Donizetti interpreted by a second-rate troupe — the *Zarzuela*, or Spanish comic opera, sung by native artists,—or, last of all, the mere amateur efforts of the English officers, laudably seeking to support the credit of our national stage.

There was great talk that December of an affair of the latter kind, and Lola had begged hard of her grandfather to be allowed to see it. Don Mariano, taking alarm, had as usual

refused, at first peremptorily, then with less
and less force, as his stern resolves faded
before our heroine's vigorous appeals. But
he resisted stoutly, till, at the last moment,
the appearance of Ramona and her brother,
who had come in unexpectedly, decided the
matter. The cousins expressed a keen desire
to see an English play, still more to see the
élite of the English garrison, and before their
entreaties Bellota was courteously compelled
to yield. A box was with difficulty procured
upon the grand tier, in front of which Ramona
and ' Lola took their seats long before the
curtain went up, and attracting no little attention as the house gradually filled. Neither
the ripe, handsome freshness of Ramona, nor
Lola's perfect features, were familiarly known,
and both were keenly examined and admired
by not a few opera-glasses in the stalls.

Frank Wriottesley came in late. Lola,
when he had spoken of this performance,
had told him there was no prospect of her
being present. Therefore he had no par-
ticular motive for attending either. But the
Sproules had a box, and pressed him to join

them during the evening. He was on his way thither, pausing first to speak to a friend or two in the stalls, when some one called his attention to "that stunning Spanish girl in the box on the grand tier."

"Lola!"

Without a moment's hesitation Frank hastened upstairs and knocked at the door of the box. Josefa's heart was in her mouth when she opened it.

"You cannot come in, Señor. This place is too public. There are here many who know us well, and the *amo* would soon hear of it. I pray you, for the love of God, retire."

But Frank would take no denial. Besides, Lola had turned her blushing face towards him, and was waving him welcome with her fan.

"At least sit here," cried Josefa, pointing to a chair near the door. "We shall be lost, undone, if you go now to the front. Wait at least till the act is over."

There was sense in what she said, and although Frank was eager, he was also circumspect at times. After all, he did not care

as yet to blazon forth too loudly the fate that
had overtaken him. It would be time enough
by and by to advertise his engagement, and
challenge criticism for the girl of his choice.
So he seated himself demurely in the back part
of the box, contenting himself with exchanging
a few words with Miguel, who was not over-
joyed to see him, and bowing pleasantly to
Ramona in return for her cordial greeting.

Presently the curtain fell. There was the
usual shuffle of the cards. People moved
from their seats, or turned to gossip with one
another. Within the first few moments Lola
changed places with Josefa.

"You said you would not come," said
Frank.

"*Como tu!*" replied Lola, pretending to
pout. "You also declared that nothing should
bring you hither. Is it thus that you behave,
hijo, when out of my sight? Which then of
all these grand proud dames had power to
tempt you break a promise made to me? Your
promises melt fast, like fat in the frying-pan."

"There is none here fit to fasten your shoe-
strings, Lola."

" *Anda!* they are English though, of your own blood. Why did you come abroad to hunt partridges in the Sierras, when there was better game close to your hand at home ? "

. " You know the saying, ' *Cual es mi tierra? la de mi mujer.'* Which is my country ? that to which my wife belongs."

" But I am not your wife," said Lola, hanging her head.

" You will be, some day."

" That will be as you behave, my son. Where do the wives come in your land over yonder ? After the horses and the dogs ? "

Lola had not read Tennyson. Her own observation of the English officers and their tastes was sufficiently close to account for this speech.

" See the curtain is up ; they are beginning again. Do you like the play ? "

" It was dull till you came. I cannot follow well ; you talk so fast, you English, yet the words can hardly come out, because you shut your teeth quite close and your lips—like this."

" Don't shut your lips, Lolita. It spoils your beauty."

" *Vaya !* Thanks for the favour you do me."

" If we were not here in public, I'd kiss you."

"*Indecente !* "- cried Lola, putting up her fan quickly with a pretty gesture between them. " Be quiet! Hush! Listen to them down there. Tell me, what are they saying, now ? "

" Shall I interpret it for you ? " said Frank earnestly, taking her hand in his. " Oh, I must indeed," he added, when she seemed to object, "I must have your hand. See, he has got her hand down there upon the stage : I must do that too if you wish me to translate."

" Yes ; but they are acting ; it is different. You must not take my hand. Paco ! They will see us ; they will indeed."

" No, they won't. There ! "

He had kissed her hand.

" It's not my fault," Frank went on, as she blushed deeply and tried to draw away. " That fellow on the stage is doing it—and badly too. Now he is saying, ' I love you, I love you ; you are the darling of my life, the starlet of my soul' "——

"It is not that. What nonsense! You are inventing."

"It is true; I swear that it is true. Those are the words he uses, only, he does not mean them—and I do."

Very pretty all this; mere silly philandering, harmless enough in itself as the cooing of turtle-doves, but in consequences more serious.

Frank flattered himself that he had escaped observation, and so, in truth, he had—except from one lynx-like pair of eyes. Mrs Sproule, seated opposite, had caught sight of a red jacket in the box with the Spanish beauties, but had no suspicion that Wriottesley was the wearer thereof. She had seen Ramona and Lola early in the evening, and remembered them both perfectly, but had not thought it necessary to bow. Her gratitude for past kindness at Agua Dulce was not keen enough to disturb her; nor did she feel there was the least necessity for making any return, even to the extent of publicly recognising the people to whom she owed so much. In her own mind she rather fancied that the kindness had been on her part in condescending to honour their house with her presence, and in accepting their very humble attentions. But while she was still wondering why Frank, faithless, had not put in an appearance at the play, she suddenly became aware that it was he who had been seated all this time in the recesses of the opposite box. Highly incensed at this desertion, she nursed her rage, and took him very seriously to task the following day.

"Well, Mr Wriottesley, I hope you are properly ashamed of yourself."

"And why?"

"Did we not keep a seat for you last night? And yet you never came."

"I was detained."

"In the opposite box only. Don't pretend you were not at the theatre, for I saw you, although you tried to hide."

"That I did not, I declare."

"When people's deeds are evil, they shun the light."

"Insinuating that my deeds are evil?"

"If the cap fits you by all means put it on."

"I have done nothing of which I need be

ashamed, Mrs Sproule. Those ladies with
whom I sat,—you know who they are, don't
you?"

"One of the girls, that sallow-faced one,
reminded me rather of the people we saw at
that Spanish farm."

" The same !"

"Common people rather. I wonder you
care to associate with them."

" They are ladies quite, Mrs Sproule.   I
cannot suffer you to say one word in their
disparagement," cried Frank rather hotly,
thereby disclosing his hand.

"Really, you must be rather hard hit to
defend them so warmly. Pray, when are we
to congratulate you ? " said Mrs Sproule with
a sneer; " and which of the two is the lucky
girl of your choice ? "

"Mrs Sproule, your question will have
to be answered some day, and I am not
ashamed to answer it now and at once. One
of those ladies I firmly intend to make my
wife."

"How romantic! And pray, how will Sir
Hector receive the news ? "

" My uncle would never say ' No '; not if he really knew Lola."

" Which is Lola? the stout or the thin one? I forget," went on Mrs Sproule, screwing up her eyes as people do when trying to remember something of very trifling importance.

"You ought not to forget her; it was she who was at so much pains to make you comfortable at Agua Dulce."

" I thought she was a sort of upper servant, and would have given her some silver, only there was not time. You cannot really mean, Mr Wriottesley, that you are serious in this?"

"Quite!"

" It seems utterly suicidal. But I know you are an obstinate man, upon whom arguments are thrown away. If you must, you must."

" And you will give me your support? I shall want the good word of a friend to bring Sir Hector round."

" You place me in a quandary, Mr Wriottesley. I cannot admit that this is the right sort of match for you, nor can I desert you in your distress. What do you wish me to do?

Call ? I will if you like; only you must tell me what are her belongings here upon the Rock; I cannot go all the way to Ximena again."

Frank, faltering a little, said, "Her name is Bellota. They live at a cottage near Rosia Bay."

" Bellota! the name seems familiar."

" Probably you have heard it before. Old Bellota is a man that every one knows."

"' The Viscount!' to be sure! What a strange coincidence! Of course, I mean that your young lady cannot be any relation of that notorious old Jew ?"

" Only his granddaughter," said Frank plump and plain. Now that he was driven into a corner he stood to his guns.

" What!" shrieked Mrs Sproule in one prolonged note of surprise. " You must be out of your mind, Mr Wriottesley."

" I am not at all out of my mind. On the contrary, Mrs Sproule, I am very sane and very positive."

" The man is not only a tradesman, but a shameless old usurer, I am told, into the bargain. It quite takes away my breath. Oh, Mr Wriottesley, you must let me say distinctly that this will never, never do for you."

. "On such a matter I must claim to be the best judge. The question affects me, and me only."

"Do you think your friends are all fools, Mr Wriottesley. If you, yourself "——

"Thank you, Mrs Sproule; pray, call me any names you like."

"We cannot suffer you to cut your own throat, I mean—not without remonstrance. Please, please be guided by advice. Do not be so wrong-headed : do not recklessly throw all your prospects away without pausing to consider what you are about to do. You can never marry a girl like this."

"Pardon me, Mrs Sproule, that is my business."

"Sir Hector will never stand it."

"That also is my business."

"Dear, dear ! have you no common sense left ? Can what is called love make big men so childish and irrational all at once ? Mr

Wriottesley, do be persuaded. By and by you would regret it—no one more. Do pause : you know the interest I have always taken in you ; forgive my speaking so plainly now. I beseech you not to sacrifice everything to this most absurd and inconsiderate passion."

"You are merely wasting words, Mrs Sproule. I have quite made up my mind."

"A more obstinate and wilful man I never met in all my life," said Mrs Sproule energetically. "But I give you up ; from this time forth I wash my hands of you."

"Do not let us part in anger, Mrs Sproule. There is much for which I have to thank you and your husband. I had hoped that now and in the future you would stand my friends."

"You will not let us," cried the lady. "We cannot encourage you in such folly as this. We cannot, in common justice, give you any advice but the very strongest entreaties to put an end to the whole affair."

"I would not go past my plighted word for all the estates in my uncle's county.

More; sooner than surrender my love for this girl I would sacrifice my right hand."

"These are mere heroics, the rhapsodies of a lunatic."

"Thank you, Mrs Sproule; then I will save you the trouble of listening longer."

"I won't detain you. I see I might as well talk to the wall."

Thus they parted, coldly, but without any actual breach; and after he was gone Mrs Sproule set to work to consider whether, in spite of all his obstinacy, she might not yet compass his deliverance from the ruin to which he was so perversely tending. She looked upon him as a man to be saved, even against his will. He was to be protected against himself, just as obstinate people are compelled, willy-nilly, to have their children vaccinated, and dirty people ought to be made to wash themselves and keep their houses clean.

Of course, she told herself, she was actuated by only the best intentions; but we know whither these good intentions lead, and beneath their fair surface other motives urged her on. She suffered not a little in temper at the obstinate opposition to her advice which Frank displayed. She was hurt at finding that she had no power to guide him; sore because it seemed that a real, wholesome passion had come to put an end to the silly Platonic affection which all along she fancied had existed between Frank Wriottesley and herself. When thus roused and egged on, Mrs Sproule was ready to go to great lengths to gain her ends. She did not recoil from measures which would have been almost loathsome to others. This match must be prevented, *coûte que coûte*, by any means, fair or foul, that promised to be efficacious. Bellota must be undeceived. No doubt he encouraged Frank Wriottesley as a great *parti* for his child. Sir Hector also must be put upon his guard; he must hear the plain truth about this lowly girl whom his nephew desired to lift into a position far above her deserts.

Mrs Sproule was not a person to leave one stone unturned in the prosecution of her resolves; her schemes should not fail for want of careful preparation; and therefore she set to work to ferret out what she could against Lola and her family, in order to give point to her arguments with Sir Hector Harrowby. In this she found a willing ally in Ciruelas, who had given her lessons on the guitar, and who gladly lent his assistance to be revenged on Frank. Through him she obtained a highly coloured account of the fate of the first Dolores, our heroine's mother, and many items of gossip which represented old Bellota in anything but a favourable light. Armed with these facts, she sent an anonymous communication to Sir Hector, which, to avoid detection, she made Ciruelas write in his own hand. By his aid she addressed old Bellota also in the same cowardly fashion.

This was the substance of the latter letter :—

"You think perhaps that in Francis Wriottesley you catch a wonderful prize for your granddaughter Lola. It is not so. He is heir to a rich man, but that man has many caprices. His first act would be to disinherit his nephew if he married beneath him, or against his uncle's consent. Take care, then, how far you suffer him to pay court to the girl. Nothing can come of it but bitter regrets, disappointments, perhaps ruin for the child I presume you love."

This missive, duly despatched, reached Don Mariano through the post. The effect it produced we will proceed to describe in the next chapter.

CHAPTER XIII.

THE LOVERS MEET AND PART.

IT would be difficult to give due effect to any description of the rage into which old Bellota fell on receipt of Mrs Sproule's letter. At first he stormed and swore, and tore his hair; loud and vigorous were his denunciations of Josefa, bitterly he upbraided Lola and the insidious scoundrel who, in spite of him, had won her affections. But as soon as the first paroxysm of passion had abated, he resolved to see his grandchild, and, taxing her openly with her fault, insist upon her renouncing her lover once and for all.

The name of Frank Wriottesley, who was mentioned in the anonymous letter, was not unknown to him. It was Bellota's business to be well acquainted with nearly all the officers of the garrison—certainly with all who, like

Frank, were noted for spendthrift tastes. Our hero had indeed done a little business already, not with Bellota himself, but with one of his agents, having required a larger sum of ready money to pay for the Bat than he could quite lay hands upon. His bills were in Bellota's strong box at Crutchett's Ramp, and the old spider had thus a certain knowledge of Frank—by simple hearsay, no more. But this raising of money was not a point to give Frank favour in Bellota's eyes, even had the old man been otherwise well disposed towards him, which he was not. Bellota's dislike of the whole class to which Frank belonged was still as strong as ever, and this underhand courtship, which had thus providentially come to light, made him if anything more bitter than before. He was resolved to put an end to the whole affair— a positive and unmistakable end.

Within an hour of the receipt of Mrs Sproule's letter he returned to Rosia Cottage, coming post-haste up the trellised verandah which led from the outer gate to the house, and making straight for the window opening on to the garden, at which his granddaughter generally sat.

Josefa, who was with her charge, crossed herself devoutly as she saw her master approach. Frank Wriottesley but a moment before had gone over the wall—his usual mode of exit.

"*El amo!* The master at this hour of the morning! But at least to-day the saints are kind. Had he seen your *novio*," she said to Lola, "not all the saints in the calendar, not Michael and all his angels, would have saved me from destruction. It puts me all in a tremble. Señorita, what evil spirit tempted you to favour this *rubio*—this mad young Englishman with his yellow hair and false blue eyes? Were there no lads, tall and brown, to take your fancy among your own people?"

"Love knows no laws, Josefyia—we are its slaves. But it is strange that *mi abuelo* should return to the house at this unusual hour."

"Some sour grape has given him the colic. He looks to have that or worse," went on Josefa, *sotto voce*, as Don Mariano came near to where they sat.

In truth, the old man's face was black,

and his eyes flashed out like storm-signals amid the dark night-clouds of an angry sky.

"Begone!" he said abruptly to Josefa. "I have that to say to this young lady which it beseems not a servant to hear."

Josefa hated to be called a servant, and it was with an unmistakable scowl that she rose and prepared to retire.

"Save your frowns, Señora of little count, you will want them ere long may be, for you and I have a settlement to make that may perchance open your flesh. Keep your back ready; there is stick enough and to spare close at hand."

Lola had been at work, and she went on stitching diligently while her grandfather was talking, seeming, with downcast eyes, to take but little notice of his words. But when he had seated himself near her, and had taken out, with the force of long habit, his tobacco-pouch and bundle of cigarette papers, she stretched out her hand towards him, saying—

"Shall I make you one?"

"*Gracias*, no," replied Don Mariano, thereby showing himself to be unusually ruffled. He loved of all things to see her make his cigarettes and light them. He loved to watch her nimble fingers, and to gaze at her bright beauty as she stood before him.

"Has some bad insect stung you, *abuelo*, that you are so cross?"

"Stung! Ay, truly am I stung, and by a poisonous asp."

"Am I the culprit? Shall I do penance with candle and book, or go to the shrine of our Lady of Europa barefoot to tell my beads by the big lighthouse that guards the Straits?"

The girl's gaiety was a trifle forced. Some misgiving seized her that her grandfather's rage was connected with Frank Wriottesley. Wrong-doers are always in momentary dread of detection. Every turn of the door-handle threatens to disclose the bearer of a forger's warrant of arrest; every footstep is that of searchers near the concealed corpse. Lola, in her little innocent way, felt herself a guilty thing, and wished now that long ere this she had made full confession of her crime— the great crime of being in love.

"Be serious, child. I am sore at heart.

Nay, more; I am enraged, furious, more savage than a bull eight years old at bay within the ring."

"And with me?" asked Lola, trembling in spite of herself. There was a curious cadence in her grandfather's voice which frightened her : she had seen him angry before, but never quite like this. "What have I done, *abuelito* of my heart? Tell me of my sin, that I may make a clean breast of it and seek absolution. Surely it is not past forgiveness?"

"Lola, as you hope for salvation, tell me, speak truly—you have a lover? No?"

She blushed scarlet, but answered saucily enough—

"*Ya lo creo.* I should think I had—a dozen. Have not all girls, save those that squint or carry humps?"

"If it were a dozen I should not mind; there is safety in crowds. But they tell me you have but one—one only—and he is not to my liking."

"Who tell you, pray? Does every gossiping dame that climbs your stony stair carry to you some new tale of me and of my doings?

Am I the talk of all those prosy knaves with whom you sit and bargain?"

"Is it true, I ask—true that you are en-meshed, entangled with one of those fiends in scarlet cloth that for some hidden purpose God suffers to walk this earth as He does the snakes and scorpions and reptiles, whom our impulse is to crush and kill lest with their venom they should do us harm? Is this true? answer me, child.. Hold up your head, and with your eyes speak as well as with your lips. Deny, for the love of Heaven —denounce this wicked, cursed lie. Tell 'me you do not love this Francis Wriottesley."

" No, *abuelo*, I cannot deny it," said Lola firmly and looking him full in the face. " For it is true, and I glory in the truth. I love him, and he loves me."

" Who is he? An officer? No?"

" Yes : I believe he is."

" You believe so! Foolish goose! Was it not the glitter of the tinsel that took you first? The coat that is not yet his own—for such as he pay no men their dues; and the gilding that is on it will tarnish like the baser metal of which his heart is made. Where didst meet him first ? "

" At San Roque."

" I feared it. That Judas, Josefa, has played me false. Oh, would that I held the power of the governor of this strong place, and I would mash her to a mummy behind this rock, and leave her till the sharks and vultures got indigestion from her foul remains."

" *Señor mio*, it was not Josefa's fault. When I fainted in the ring it was he who carried me out; and then in the evening, at the Casino—we danced."

" Who took him there ? "

" Miguel."

" Holy sainted men ! but every hand was against me. Fate is hard to fight. And since then you have met often ? "

" At Agua Dulce; he came thither to buy horses."

" And here, in this house, upon the public walks, where ? Don't hang your head. Can I not guess ? Shame on you, mild-eyed and gentle-voiced but deceitful and double-faced child ! But as for Josefa, sourest locust of this season, she shall smart, I say. And you, Lola, you must give him up. Nay, seek not to alter my resolve. You must and shall forget him and promise me never to see him more."

"I will not," replied Lola with decision. Then suddenly changing her tone she cried, "Oh, do not say you will separate us for ever, *abuelo mio!* It would be my death."

And she fondled him and made much of him, as women will—even the purest and best —to stave off sentence and gain their ends.

Don Mariano held her from him at arms-length and spoke slowly—

"Maria de los Dolores—Our Lady of Sorrows—thus were you named at birth. Know'st why?"

"It was my mother's name. No?"

"There was yet another reason than that."

Bellota paused; he hated to tear up the hard ground, the crust beneath which, far down, his griefs were buried though still alive. But with a strong effort he continued—

"Listen, Lola; I will tell you a tale, as often I have romanced to amuse you, when, almost a babe, you sat prattling and laughing on

my knee. There was a man once—no matter
when—happy in the love of a devoted wife,
surrounded by a host of little ones whom
the good God had given him. He was
poor—what matter? Returning when his
day's toil was done, a dozen merry tongues
greeted his approach; the good wife soothed
his brow, and upon his own peaceful hearth
he forgot his troubles, and gained fresh courage to struggle for their daily bread. Suddenly, in one short moment, so it seemed,
there came a blight—a plague fell upon
him. His saints forgot to speak for him,
their shrines perchance had been neglected—
perchance our Holy Mother looked away,
and without her sheltering grace the Evil
One had power to work his will. At one
stroke, at one fell swoop, in one short
summer's night, he lost them all, but one—
all that he held most dear,—the wife he
adored, the children of his loins,—all dead,
dead of the same fell fever—the yellow plague.
Ah, God! how well I remember now."—As
he grew more impassioned, the flimsy pretence
of speaking at second-hand vanished, and it

became clear that it was his own story that he told. "How well I remember each fatal blow. I knew the disease by heart, and could detect it as it crept towards them with stealthy step, noting each symptom, unmasking every move, till hope was lost and all was done. Nine blessings I once possessed, and eight were gone. One alone remained—saved, as I think, by the intercession of those others already gathered up to glory. She, by the mercy of Heaven, was spared, to be, as I fondly hoped, some consolation in my terrible grief. In her alone I lived. There was none to compare with her, as she grew up, gracious and beautiful, a gift received direct from Heaven. It is of your mother, Lola, that I speak."

"And what became of her, *abuelo*. You never spoke like this before,—tell me what happened my sweet mother? (May she rest in peace l)"

"She was as the apple of my eye. I think I would have sold my soul to bring one gleam of pleasure to her cheek. I had nursed and tended and loved her from a child; and yet, and yet"——

"Yes, yes! go on."

"She left me without a word—deserted me, her father, to follow the fortunes of a scoundrel who dazzled her by the deceitful light he flashed in her eyes like a will-of-the-wisp or corpse-candle, luring her only to her ruin.   I went up one morning, as was my wont, with a dish of the fruit she loved. Her room was empty; she was gone.   Gone! O God! I thought I should have died!'

He paused for breath, consumed by strong emotion ; then broke out into sudden maledictions—

"May Heaven's curse wither him and blast him still.   But he is dead ; he died soon afterwards, leaving her forsaken, also to die.   His grand relations took no heed.   Who was she ? A light, wanton girl, full of the warm Southern blood, whose passionate affection had been beyond control.   They would not recognise her ; nay, they drove her from them ; and she came back to me, wasted and worn, the shadow of her former self—she returned to me, her father, whom one short year before she had deserted without remorse or shame."

"But say, *abuelo*, say quickly, you did not reject her, you did not turn her, poor darling, from your door?"

"I was not inhuman, Lola. The tigers suckle their whelps. She was the last of nine who had called me father; she was of my flesh and blood; for their sake and hers I took her in, and did my best to nurse the pale flame of life which had flickered already down so low. But alas! our blessed sun was not strong enough to thaw the chilling frosts of the inhospitable North. She died—as you were born, Dolores. Dolores! child of my innermost heart, she died and left me too!"

Very poignant and bitter was the old man's grief even now as he re-told the story of his sorrow. Great tears were rolling down his hard and wrinkled cheeks, and his brow was deeply marked by the pain he suffered.

Our Dolores, Dolores the younger, was silent. What indeed could she say? This terrible story was quite new to her. Its sad details went straight to her heart. She grieved for the lost mother she had never known, but she had no apprehensions for herself. She need not distrust her Frank. That pretty confidence which all girls possess in the man on whom they doat, convinced our Lola that with Frank Wriottesley her happiness was perfectly secure. If her grand-father did but know him! Full of this thought, she stole her hand gently towards his, and following it, seated herself, childlike, upon the old man's knee.

"*Abuelo, abuelito*, I would cut off my hair and cast it in the gutter sooner than give you pain. There would be no joy for me in life if you were sorrowful and sad—nothing would tempt me from your side. I do not dream of leaving you—nor does my Francisco wish it. He"——

"Is a lying thief—a villain who steals in unawares to rob a better man of his choicest jewel."

"No, grandfather! Paco is as honest as the sun, and as good as he is true. He would scorn to do a dirty deed."

"What call you this clandestine plucking of the turkey, then? Is it not mean and underhand to pay you court and say no word to me?"

" Would you have received him, *abuelo*, if he had asked your permission first ? "

This was a home thrust.

" That is past now. It is too late to speak of that. He did not give me the chance. I have sworn an oath that you shall never fall into the clutches of such a man as he. We may be fallen low in the world, but our sense of shame is not less keen on that account."

" What shame, then ? Can there be any shame in such love as his ? I pride in it, as I do in the prospect of being one day called his wife."

" His wife ! Child, it is plain that you know little of this wicked world, still less of him who flatters your foolish heart with honied words. Think you it is his purpose to wed you, to put you on a level with himself and the cold proud people of his class ? Lola ! innocent, guileless child, you may thank God that your eyes have not been opened too late to the fraud and falsehood which are as the breath in the nostrils of such men as he."

" You do him foul wrong, grandfather,"

cried Lola with wide flashing eyes. Wonder at Bellota's words had opened them first, and now indignation followed to give them a keener fire. " See here is his ring ; he has pledged me his troth. He has sworn that I, and I alone, shall be his wife."

" Words, idle words! His deceitful, lying tongue can coin them as fast as a Jew doubloons."

" Paco tells no lies."

" We shall see. At least he does not tell you *all* the truth."

" How know you that ? What remains for him to tell ?" inquired Lola artlessly.

" Does he tell you of his house, of his relatives, away beyond there in rich, proud England ? "

" He has told me that his parents are dead ; that they lost their lives in a fatal shipwreck."

" Ay! but has he spoken of that uncle to whom he is fast bound, hand and foot, owing him everything in this world ? "

" Yes ; I know him by heart, and the house in which he lives, and which will be Francisco's too some day."

" And yours also ? Is it so foolish an idiot?

God makes it easy for the fool to swallow. Half such a pill would stick in my dry throat. That house is not his."

" But it will be."

" Never ; not if he marries with such as you. Of this I have good proof. His uncle would probably disinherit him if he took home any bride not of the old man's choosing ; but assuredly if he demeaned himself to wed with a Bellota—though our ancestors were kings when his yet tilled the soil. If you married him you would but disgrace and ruin him." •

"I would die first!" cried Lola. "But he never told me this. O grandfather, is it really true ?"

"I have it on the best authority—a letter from a friend."

" May I ask him ? Let him but tell me with his own lips that I stand between him and fortune, and there will be no necessity for your stormy words. I would give him up of my own free will."

" You shall see him. But trust not to what he says. He will truckle and dissemble, as lying villains always do," cried Bellota, still beside himself with rage.

" Methinks this unmeasured abuse comes but ill from you, *abuelo*, who owest him, if not your life, at least escape from serious harm."

" I owe him ? Girl, are you mad ?"

" Did you not go on board the ship that brought him out, and did not the rude sentry seek to stay your steps with rough handling and coarser words ? Who saved you then ? You never knew ? Paco, my Paquito, who has told me the story again and again, for I loved to hear that he was kind and generous, and could stoop to protect the aged when per-secuted and in trouble. And this is the only return you make him—abuse, cruel abuse !"

Lola's words staggered the old man not a little. He was silent; then with a heavy sigh, he rose, saying, " My oath ! my oath !" and went into the house.

How the poor child fought and wrestled with herself that night ! It was now, for the first time, that she really missed a mother's love—the true shield for a maiden's guileless heart. Out of the fulness of her own expe-rience the tender parent guides her daughter's feelings, administering gentle reproof if needed,

soft sympathy, or that healing consolation
which binds up the . sorest wounds. Such
cordial kindness, such rich affection, Lola had
never known. She had now no refuge in
her distress, no close and bosom friend to
whom she could fly to pour out all her woes.
She felt alone in the world, and conscious
that she must decide for herself this knotty
question, wherein lay the first real difficulty
and trial in.all her hitherto happy joyous life.

It touched her so nearly! If disappointed
now, it seemed as if her whole future must
be tainted with the black and bitter grief.
Was it possible, she asked herself, to give up
her. Frank, her treasure, the rich possession
in which were concentrated all ideas of happiness now and to come? And yet, to keep
him would be at the price of his own ruin.
Could she with such utter selfishness ruin all
his worldly prospects? For, if her grandfather's story were true, it amounted to this;
and the fear of doing her lover any injury,
the mere notion of standing in his light, when
duly realised, threatened to outweigh all other
considerations. No; a thousand times better

to lose him than to bring him into misery and
disgrace. But for this she would have never
despaired. Her grandfather's opposition could
not be quite insuperable. Had she not already
talked the old man out of 'refusals more peremptory than this ? His obstinacy, as we
know, had never prevailed long against the
persistence of her attacks, backed up with all
the argument that lay in her pleading voice
and winning ways. Might she not once more
overcome his scruples ? Yes ; if that were all,
there might have been hope ; but there could
be no hope if these crossgrained relatives in
England were really so disagreeable and hard.

And at length out of all her long and tearful
self-communings came this decision, that she
would obtain confirmation of her fears, or the
reverse, from the lips of her lover himself,

When Frank came next day to the garden,
she received him coldly enough.

"It is an age since we met, *vida mia* (my
life)," cried impetuous Frank, seeking to en-
fold her at once in his arms.

"Back ; do not touch me."

"You are not usually so shy, my soul's
planet. In what have I displeased you ?"

"Sit there—on that far sofa—a long way off. Yes; it is my order; sit as I desire you."

"Are we going to play at soldiers?"

"There is no. joke or play in what I am going to say to you. Paco, you must be very formal—you must. I have much to ask, and our talk must be serious—very serious."

"But you love me still? Do not deny your creed."

"We shall see—it depends. There! sit still, do. Wait where you are, my son, and tell me quickly,—who are you?"

Frank laughed aloud.

"This is a court of justice, then, and you are to try me in the balance? Be merciful, most righteous judge!"

"It will be as you answer, culprit. Are you not very wicked? You should be hung in chains, and sent to work at Ceuta. But now try and speak the truth. Tell me, I ask again, who are you?"

"My name is Francis Wriottesley; my friends call me Frank. My Lola says Paquito. My hair is light, my eyes green; I have two of them, item two arms, item two legs"——

" So has a goose, my friend. But this is not to the purpose. Where do you come from ? Where is your home—the house of your friends ? "

" At Grimswych. I told you of that long ago."

" And you live—how ? "

" How I can—without you, that is to say."

" Does your life depend upon me then ? "

" You know it does—my life and my happiness."

" What is your idea of happiness, Paco ? Stay ! let me ask you—you know my cousins' farm at Agua Dulce. There by the mill stream stands a little hut of reeds, where lives the man who feeds Teresa's pigs. His name is Sebastian Barsé—a worthy man, too, who supports his wife and ten little ones on only a few farthings a day. Tell me, could you live on bread and oil, and a few farthings a day ? "

" With you, certainly."

" And the pigs ? "

" Your Spanish pigs are dear black balls, and cleaner than many Christians. What pleasanter existence than feeding the pigs, and my

Lola to bring the acorns. You would bring my dinner too, a bowl of *gazpacho*."

"Which you know you cannot eat, and always call pigs' food."

"Well, then, they could have it, and I the acorns; or you would give me a fowl boiled in rice, or a salad of oranges and saffron, or some broth of yellow beans. What would it matter if you yourself cooked it?"

"You would live thus, you, my fine *caballero*, with your nice English ways, your comforts, and your luxuries? You would be ready to face penury, and squalor and trials?"

"If needs be, yes; and more, to gain you."

"And does it not amount to this, Francisco? To marry me would be to make yourself an outcast from your people. No?"

"Oh, no, my beautiful bird! *Now* I see what you are driving at."

"But, yes; I say. You see I know all about you—that you have an uncle rich as all the Indies—a hard cold man, an English *milor*, with no sympathy for such as me and mine— who would not suffer you to fall so low as to wed with the grandchild of a man who keeps a

shop.   Is not this so? Would your uncle
consent to such a bride as me ? "

" My uncle is anxious I should settle. He
wishes me to be married."

" To me ? "

" To you, my child—at least, he would if
he knew you." Frank could not help fencing
a little. He was too honest to deceive Lola
wilfully, yet the insinuations dropped by Mrs
Sproulè had set him thinking, and he was far
from confident that the way to happiness would
at first be quite smooth and clear of obstacle.

" Ay, wicked ! have I caught you ?   He
does not know me.   How then ? "

Frank was for the moment " posed."   He
could not reply all at once.

" Listen   to   me,   Paco—Francisco,   whom
God and the Virgin know I love, ay, more
than I do my own soul, may I be forgiven for
saying so.   I would die, die the death of all the
martyrs, rather than stand in the way between
you and all your people. Yes, you might cut
me into little pieces as they did the blessed
St Christopher, or grill me on a gridiron like
the holy St Lawrence, before I would "——

" Stay, stay, Lola ; you are too fast "——

" Listen first to me, Francisco. Nothing, I say, would induce me to act as the bitter pill for your English friends to swallow ; " and then, stamping her foot with increasing vehemence, as the question presented itself to her in a new light, she went on, " and have we no pride, do you suppose ? We Bellotas have blood as blue, ay bluer, than yours. We are sons and daughters of some one (*hidalgos*), and our ancestors two genera- tions back were grandees of Spain. We may be poor and fallen now. My father sells you what you wish, and I am but an ignorant underbred child ; still "——

" Why, Lola, you are fit to be a duchess."

" Thank you for the honour you do me."

"I wish to heaven I were a duke for your sake. You should be a duchess then I swear."

" You are my Paco—ah ! if only you might be—and that would be quite enough for me."

" Come, Lolita, you are more reasonable now. You have been jesting so far, you have not said all this in real earnest. No- thing would make you forget your promise ? "

"I know that I can never love again;
that the world holds one man only 'for me;
that, if I cannot have my Paco, no one else
will do.   But understand me, plain, plain;
you shall not win me, never, never, never,
unless your friends agree."

" Must they come and ask you ? "

" Yes ; at least I must know that they
wish me to be your wife.   I am resolved,
Francisco, I am by my salvation and the
sweet Virgin Mother."

" Then my uncle shall ask you himself."

" You will write and get his consent? O son
of my soul, write, and write words that would
have persuaded the crucifying Jews to hold
their murderous hands.   Write as if all the
universe were in feud till that answer came.   It
is in truth my world which is bounded in that
letter, and if it fails—the great and awful day,
the last, may come, I care not how soon."

Poor child ! she was wound up to so high
a pitch, that the strings cracked, as it were,
and all at once her strength gave way.   With
a loud torrent of sobs she fell almost sense-
less into Wriottesley's arms.   If Frank had

needed proof of the absorbing character of the passion she felt for him, her last words, and the grief that followed, would have been more than enough to convince him. But indeed he had never doubted her love; and the only effect of the scene in which he was now taking part was to intensify and deepen his own. Strangely affected, as true men will be at the evidence of devotion to themselves, he was powerless to check her tears or to assuage her grief; and could only kiss her wet cheek again and again, murmuring in her ear all the soft endearing words of a language rich in tender expressions. " My heart's life," " starlet of my soul," " precious jewel."

But Lola soon recovered herself.

" You will write, Paco ? "

" At once."

" And will show me his answer ? "

" Yes."

" Whichever way it is ? "

" It can only be one answer. He has but to know you, and he could not hold out a single instant. But what has led to all this ? Who has told you of my uncle ? "

" My own grandfather."

" Don Mariano ! then he *knows ?* "

" Everything.   How, I cannot tell; but
you remember how unexpectedly he returned
yesterday?   He came in here, just as you had
gone, and taxed me straight with encouraging
your attentions.   I did not deny it."

" And then ? "

" He commanded me to give you up.   I
refused; and then he told me a story—a sad,
sad story—of a girl like me, here upon this
big Rock, who, alas! for her, attracted the
attention of one, an officer, an English officer
here, it may be such as you are, my Paco.
She fled with her lover, deserting her
father—an unfortunate, who had no other
child alive—fled, to find herself one day
neglected, scouted, abandoned, left alone,
perhaps to die upon a foreign inhospitable
shore.   Francisco, that girl was my mother."

" Gracious God! Lola, do you deem me
capable too of such villany as this ?   If so,
we had better part to-day, this hour."

" Have I said I doubted you ?   No, Paco,"
said Lola, drawing herself up proudly to her

full height. "I have that faith and trust in you, my heart's choice, that I would go forth this instant, my hand in thine, out upon the wide, wide world, freely confiding in thy honour as I do in my own."

"And she was your mother! Did you know her?"

"She died as I was born. But you cannot wonder now that my grandfather should detest the class to which you belong, and that he should refuse to entertain your suit."

"He knows I am a gentleman."

"Yes; and for that reason distrusts your intentions. But even that I could overcome. My *abuelo* is not proof against my coaxing;" and once again she broke into her merry laugh. "And he felt he was not safe, so he played a stronger card—your uncle."

"And yet we will beat it. I will write to-night a letter that would melt a stone."

"You think you will succeed?"

"I am sure of it."

"Then go and write; do not delay."

"In fourteen days at latest the answer will be here. Then I will beard Don Mariano in his own den, and marry you in spite of him and all the world."

"Fourteen days—it seems an age. And not to see you all that time !"

"How ? "

"My grandfather has forbidden me to see you ever again. This meeting he knows of, and allowed, on condition only that it should be the last. He threatens to set a watch on me, and that if we are found together he will send me to a convent in the North of Spain."

"And yet we shall meet again, Lolita, I think—once again, at least."

"Only once !" cried Lola pouting.

"Yes, once ; but that will be for always."

And with this for the present they parted.

END OF VOL. I.

Lightning Source UK Ltd.
Milton Keynes UK
UKHW021316250219
337978UK00013B/1786/P